EMINENT DOMAIN

INDIGORIVER
PUBLISHING

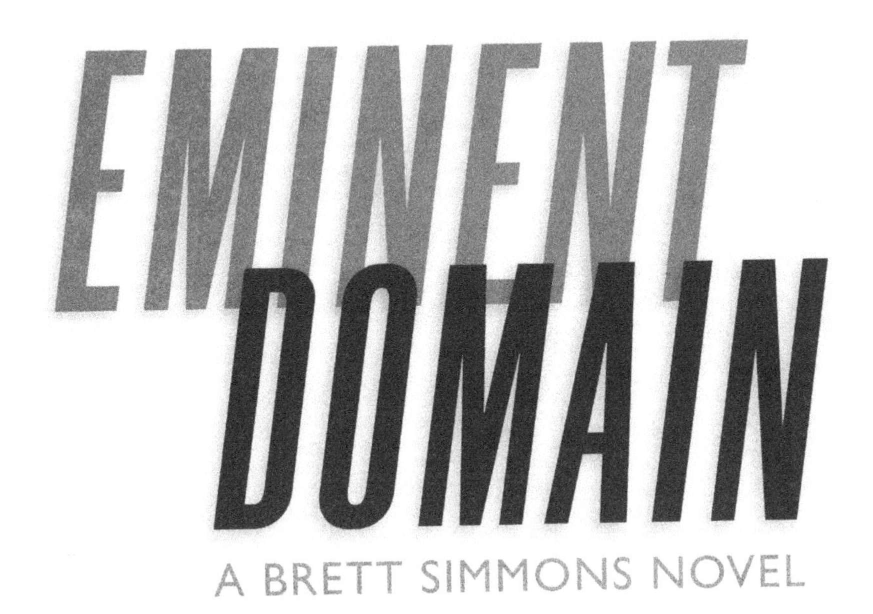

RONALD D. DEMMANS

Indigo River Publishing
3 West Garden Street, Ste. 718
Pensacola, FL 32502
www.indigoriverpublishing.com

First edition, 2022
Printed in the United States of America

Eminent Domain | Ronald D. Demmans, author
LCCN 2021918609 | ISBN 978-1-954676-22-0

Cover and Interior design by Emma Grace
Author Photography by Freeman Renaissance Castle Portraits

To:

Janet, Adam, and Alex

and

Carmen and Primrose

em·i·nent do·main

noun

the right of a government or its agent to expropriate private property for public use, with payment of compensation

PROLOGUE

THANKS FOR THE OPPORTUNITY to share my side of the story. Up until now I have been unable to talk about certain incidents, under threat of severe consequences, but over the past few months events have taken place that will allow me to discuss virtually everything that happened. It's been almost a year and a half, and the dust has pretty much settled. I'll tell you what I know about the situations that led up to my involvement in the affair, and the final outcome, of which you probably have some idea. I'll leave it up to you to decide if I'm credible and if what I tell you is the truth.

Before I start, I need to issue a disclaimer, a warning if you like. I have a split personality. But I'm not in Sybil's league. I just have two. If you were to ask my friends, they might tell you I can be somewhat of a smart-ass. As sobering as this story is, there are times, mostly on an involuntary basis, I'll allow levity to overtake gravity. Describing me as irreverent wouldn't be inaccurate. But I also have this internal switch that I don't control. At a moment's notice I can go from the wisecracking jokester, make a 180-degree turn, and become a serious sonofabitch lawyer, taking no prisoners. I guess what they say about Geminis is true. Both of me would concur.

Things really took off because of two innocuous words of legalese. Just two. Get comfortable; it's a rather convoluted story that takes place over several years. I think it's best if I start at the beginning.

My name is Brett Simmons. I'm a lawyer. Self-employed, a sole practitioner for most of my professional life. I grew up in Lenore, at least until my junior year of high school. Lenore is Hoosier country. You can find us in the southernmost part of Indiana, halfway between Evansville and Louisville, about a three hours' drive down from Indianapolis. My father was transferred literally across the country. He got a promotion and a significant raise. It was absolutely the right thing for him to do, but at the time, as a seventeen-year-old, I didn't think so. Devastated would aptly describe my emotional state. I had to leave my friends, the ones I had grown up with; my grandparents on my father's side, with whom I spent more time than at home; and, most importantly, Mallory McCutcheon, the love of my life, or so I thought. She was heartbroken for at least forty-eight hours, and that's when Steve Halson asked her out. I'm not sure I ever got over it. But that's another story.

There were some heroes in my life. My dad and my mother, each in their own way. They raised six children, teaching us independence and the value of hard work while allowing us to pursue our individual dreams, whatever they might be. We didn't always get what we wanted, but we always had what we needed. My grandmother was a jewel, a godly woman. She taught me grace under fire, and what Christian values I have today came mostly from her. But I'm afraid I never mastered her belief in turning the other cheek. Then there was my grandfather. He taught me so much, like how to change a tire and the difference between a Phillips-head and a slotted screwdriver. But the things I cherish the most: he taught me that character is what you are when you think no one is looking; that personal integrity, though seldom free, should stand above all else. And just as important: personal accountability—taking responsibility for your actions. On yet another level, he taught me the art of swearing. Not just the words themselves, but what words to use in which situations, his version of PC, the protocol of cussing. As I proceed with my story, many of the things he taught me will become evident. I hope I do him proud! By the way, he also showed me how to chew tobacco. I never caught on to that skill. After my first session I threw up for like three days, hurling things I had eaten at least six months before. Never touched the stuff again, which was probably his plan all along. I miss him. I think about him every day. But I do feel his presence.

So I confidently, if not naively, entered adulthood fully armed, or so I believed, against anything life would throw at me.

A major influence in my young life was our family doctor, Robert McHugh. I loved that man. He put eight stitches in my leg and four above my left eye. You can barely see the scar. He cauterized a blood vessel in my nose, several times. He signed off on my physical so I could play safety for the Lenore High School football team, at 135 pounds, soaking wet, in pads. The way people spoke about him made it sound like he was headed for sainthood, and I wanted to be just like him. That was, until I ran headlong into math and science. They were not my friends, nor would they ever be. My biology teacher once described trying to teach me botany and zoology was like trying to flog a dead horse. That was the attaboy I needed. One rainy Saturday afternoon, with my grass-cutting chores postponed and little else to do, I watched a marathon of old Perry Mason shows. I was on to something. After four years of undergraduate studies, where I learned the complexities of competitive beer drinking, three more years of law school, where I further honed my beer-drinking proficiency, I ended up right back where I started. My parents had arranged for me to join the public defender's office in my adopted hometown. Nope. I wanted to come back to Lenore. All of my childhood friends had escaped from Lenore, never to return again. Not me. Although not quite as dramatic as the Prodigal Son, I came back. Probably a shrink would tell you that I chose Lenore because I wanted to show Mallory McCutcheon what I had become. There might be some truth to that.

I was introduced to Jimmy Hollins, my grandfather's lawyer. We hit it off. His practice was expanding and I needed a job. It was a good fit, as they say. I started my law career in a tiny, windowless office that had once been a storage closet, at 310 West Main Street, which runs into Lenore's town square, which is really a circle. The sign out front read, "James B. Hollins and Associates, Attorneys-at-Law." The James was Jimmy of course, and I correctly assumed the "Associates," plural, was me.

Life was good. I met Sarah at a library fundraiser. At first I thought she was snooty, beautiful, but a little full of herself, and later she told me she thought I was a bit of a buffoon. I was totally wrong about her other than the fact she was indeed beautiful. But her assessment of me was right on the money. I asked her out twice that evening. I got a no both times. I heard somewhere that the third time's a charm. Nope. It was a few weeks later that I was having lunch at the Chelsea, alone, when she stopped at my table and, to my surprise, asked if she could join me. Apparently, there were no tables available and she didn't want to wait. I guess my table was the least offensive of the other choices she had. About halfway through the meal, the buffoon in me rose to the surface and I asked her, since this was our first date, would she have dinner with me for our second. It must have totally stunned her because she said yes, but only if she could choose the restaurant. I agreed. And from that day forward, our choice of eateries rested squarely on her shoulders.

Marital bliss lasted about two years, give or take. She was into most things I wasn't. Like sushi, chick flicks and yoga, just to name a few. There was little mutual interest in each other's careers. I guess our parting of the ways was inevitable. I found out that opposites do attract, but not permanently. I also found out, through an anonymous note left under the windshield wiper blade of my '72 Plymouth Duster, that the frequent trips she was taking to her hometown of Wendover, to visit her sick grandmother, were simply opportunities to shack up with her former high school sweetheart. Sadly, I never got that chance with Mallory McCutcheon. But I digress. Apparently, Sarah and the co-respondent, as he was called in the divorce hearing, rekindled the old flame at a high school reunion. They have three kids and are living happily ever after. In hindsight, I can say better him than me.

Although the split with Sarah stung a little, felt mostly by my ego, I recovered quickly and moved on. I wasn't about to become a monk living a vow of celibacy in a mountaintop monastery. Nope. Unlike Humpty Dumpty, I was able to put the pieces back together and commit all my energies to becoming a better advocate for my clients. I was well on my way to making that happen when, for whatever reason, I inadvertently took a look behind the curtain. Not just any curtain. The wrong one. I saw things I shouldn't have seen and soon found myself embroiled in a conspiracy that would take me down a dangerous path of lies, deceit, and murder.

This is a story of a small town and one lawyer's crusade to preserve its innocence. This is my story and it's time for me to tell it.

CHAPTER 1

WHAT LENORE WAS AND what the town has become is critical to the story. For me, my town was Mayberry. We didn't have an Andy Taylor, but we did have Barney Fife. More than one. For generations, Lenore was a lazy bedroom town about thirty-five miles from the bustling metropolis of King City, the seat for the mostly agricultural county of Dunham, one of ninety-two counties in Indiana. I was a villager, which meant I grew up within the boundaries of the original village of Lenore, founded in 1871. Being called a villager was not always a compliment, particularly coming from the rich folks who lived in the newer, more affluent subdivisions that seemed to be springing up everywhere. As King City grew, so did Lenore. We used to walk the old radial car tracks from the south end of town all the way north to Riddell Road, near the school. The radial car service ended in the 1930s. The new railroad—citing a lack of economic viability—didn't come this far, at least not until Westlake Industries purchased several hundred acres of farmland northeast of town and built a huge factory some seventy years later. Westlake apparently signed a multimillion-dollar deal with the air force to supply military aircraft parts. The land was cheap, the railroad was willing to extend its line beyond King City, and, just as importantly, Lenore was advertised as a great place to live and raise a family. Amen to that!

Unfortunately, along with all that growth came changes that were not always well received by the townsfolk. Big-box stores, endless rows of townhouses, apartment complexes, older buildings being torn down and new buildings going up everywhere you looked, which takes us to our first scandal. Well, maybe not the first in the town's history, but the first that involved an attorney named Brett Simmons. That would be me.

The mayor at the time, Martin Young, was thrilled about Westlake, the air force, and all the trappings. It meant growth, which in turn meant a bigger tax base and therefore more of other people's money he and his cronies could spend. There were no term limits for mayor in Lenore. For two successive elections, his fifth and sixth terms, he took credit for putting the deal together, which of course was total nonsense, and most people knew it. The only thing he got involved in was the ground-breaking and the ribbon-cutting ceremonies. Come election time there weren't any races for mayor of Lenore. No one chose to run against him.

So, where does Brett Simmons fit in?

First, I'll give you a brief résumé of my law career. I had a marvelous relationship with my partner, Jimmy Hollins. Don't read too much into that. I never got the chance to make full partner. We had a great five-year run together, with partnership imminent, practicing all kinds of law. We represented clients in real estate, civil, corporate, criminal, and juvenile law. And speaking of juvenile, I was still "and Associates" when our long-time juvenile court judge, Livingston Metcalfe, was caught with his hand in the cookie jar. Actually, it was another part of his anatomy that was caught, and he wasn't going for Oreos. He had given a pretty juvenile offender probation along with community service, which turned out to be servicing His Honor.

Her parents found out and there he stood, with his pants around his ankles, figuratively speaking. She was only fifteen, which is the time we all figured he'd get after he pleaded guilty. He got only nine years. He was out in six, never to be heard from again.

The state AG's office, that being the attorney general, offered the position on the bench to one James B. Hollins. In my humble opinion they didn't always make wise choices, but in this case they did, given Jimmy's experience in juvenile law and his overall high regard in the community. And he also made the wise choice to accept. So, where did that leave me? For one, I could no longer practice juvenile law in Judge Jimmy's courtroom. Conflict of interest and all that. I was left as a sole practitioner in this grand profession. The best part for me was that I was able to convince my assistant, Emma Roberts, whom I addressed as Peel, to stay with me. I was in love with Diana Rigg, who played Emma Peel on the Avengers in the '60s—my favorite era. So Peel it was and is. If she had a problem with it, she never said.

I recognized early on that I needed Peel more than she needed me. I learned about the law and courtroom protocol from Jimmy. More than was ever taught at law school. And I will forever be grateful to him. But it was Peel who educated me on how to run a law office; how a small-town law office is supposed to appear, particularly from our clients' perspective; and most importantly what it shouldn't look like. I envisioned taking up my lofty position behind a highly polished cherry desk about the size of an aircraft carrier, with a matching credenza. My chair would be plush, in black leather, and when I sat down, I would sink into its richness while still retaining that height advantage over my clients seated on the other side of the USS *Brett Simmons.* The visitor chairs would be red leather Queen Anne chairs.

Nope.

Peel found an adequately sized oak desk, used. My chair was one of those ergonomic jobs with far too many buttons and knobs. Used. The credenza almost matched. Again, used. She found my visitor chairs, which had probably graced a doctor's office several years or decades earlier, at a flea market. I wanted an in tray and an out tray. "Too trashy looking," she said. I wanted sophisticated elegance but she argued for understated functionality. I treated clients' files a little too casually, according to Peel. She would rescue those documents and place them in the filing cabinets so they could be easily accessed the next time. My name was on the sign, but it was Peel's show. She was the driver and I was just a passenger along for the ride, from the very beginning of our venture together, and I wouldn't have had it any other way.

The Office of Brett Simmons, Esq., was located at 160 North Bridge Street, on the first floor of an older two-story building, conveniently within walking distance of the courthouse, which also housed the municipal offices. Peel and I occupied suite 104. The term "suite" might be a stretch. As you entered the reception area your eyes would immediately find Peel's desk—a hand-me-down from Jimmy's office. To the right of her desk a short hallway led to my office, the small conference room, and the kitchen area. The bathroom facility was next to the rear door. Initially I thought of the place as small and cramped. Eventually I found it to be quaint and cozy, the perfect place for a small-town lawyer. Kudos again to Peel.

The paint on my custom-made shingle was barely dry and there was nothing but vacancies in my appointment book when my first client came into my office. Apparently, he didn't feel the need for an appointment, and although there was no sign indicating walk-ins were welcome, at this stage I was fine with that. It was late on a Friday. Peel and I were winding down after a not-so-hectic week of providing the good citizens of Lenore with expert legal help, of which so far no one had taken advantage. And legally, of course, I was not allowed to say that I was an expert at anything. So, when I say it, that's just between you and me.

I remember the look on her face when she came into my office.

"Mr. Simmons, there's someone here to see you."

"Peel, why are you calling me Mr. Simmons?"

She whispered, "He might be a client."

I was unable to mask my enthusiasm. "Well then, show him in."

The man was obviously a blue-collar type. A beige work shirt with that little opening down the side of the pocket where you can put one of those oversized carpenter pencils, dark brown cargo pants, and not-so-new work boots, probably steel-toed. He stood maybe six feet tall or a little more, with a high and tight military haircut. He was about thirty years old.

We shook hands. "I'm Brett Simmons. How can I help you?"

"I own a business and I want to incorporate, or whatever you call it."

"We can certainly do that for you. How did you hear about us?"

That was the royal "us," of course.

"My wife knows Judge Hollins's daughter, Meghan. She recommended you."

I would call Meghan later and thank her. I must confess, I had a thing for Jimmy's youngest daughter. She was beautiful. Still is. The problem was that I was treated like family, which would make her my almost sister and, with all the impure thoughts I had about her, makes it the nearest thing to incest. Yikes, I knew I was going straight to hell.

I asked him some background questions, he wrote me a check for $900, and in about a week or so I caused my first client to be incorporated. Of course, the $900 would barely put a dent into what I had spent on the office, the furniture, the fax, the phones—all the stuff successful law offices need. But it was a start.

I didn't know if I'd ever see Client 1 again. I hoped he'd need further legal services down the road. He came back much sooner than I thought. Turned out he needed help barely a month later.

* * *

"I need to talk to somebody, Mr. Simmons." He looked scared.

"Are you in any trouble?" I noticed small beads of sweat forming on his upper lip.

"Not sure. It's really a situation that I don't know how to handle."

"What you say here stays here." I could have quoted attorney-client privilege to him, but I didn't want to muddy the waters. He looked confused enough.

"Thanks. I'm working on a very nice project. I'm building a pool house for a client. Because it's a separate building from the house and has plumbing and electricity, I need the building inspector to give it the OK."

So why would he need legal help?

"Simple enough, so what's the issue?"

"I was having lunch at the Shack today with another contractor and told him that it's been almost two weeks and I can't get the building inspector out to see the project. So he asked me if I had greased the skids. I guess I gave him the deer-in-the-headlights look because he said that it was common practice to give a small donation—under the table of course—to the building inspector's retirement fund. Then he winked at me."

I didn't like where this was going. Not one bit.

"A bribe?"

He nodded. "I guess that's what it is. Like a hundred or two hundred dollars, depending on the size of the project."

I told him to lay low for a few days while I did some research.

I went to see Judge Jimmy. I needed his advice. This was extortion and here in our little town of Lenore, as in most towns, that's illegal.

And what's more, here's this young man, trying to get his business off the ground, and these guys—who are supposed to be in a position of trust—were simply ripping him off. Nope. Not in my town, fellas. I knew my grandfather was looking down at me, smiling.

With Jimmy's support, I contacted the state AG's office. Probing municipal corruption was in their jurisdiction. In a few weeks we had a full-blown investigation of the building inspector's office. I stayed out of the way. The investigator had also brought along an IRS agent for good measure. Client 1 agreed to wear a wire, and along with the cash being in marked bills, the transaction was recorded, both audio and video. The Perp—as we say in the business—was caught red-handed.

After he was arrested, he did three things: First, he cried like a baby as he wet himself. Then he admitted to corruption, among other things. And finally, he named all the other co-conspirators. So why is this little blemish on the legacy of Lenore so important? In addition to our friends in the building inspector's office, our illustrious mayor, Martin Young—whose name also appeared on the infamous building inspector's list—was indicted. I guess the mayor's salary wasn't enough to maintain the lifestyle that he and his wife had envisioned when he was first elected. His palms were as greasy as the burgers at Wally's Drive-In, which, by the way, are my favorite.

With Mayor Marty's untimely departure, Lenore was in the market for a new leader.

CHAPTER 2

SO HOW DID THE exit-in-disgrace of Mayor Marty affect me? I mean, it shouldn't have. The problem for me was that our mayor chose to plead not guilty, unlike the others. His defense was that the good folks over at the building inspector's office were simply making donations to his re-election campaign fund. Uh-huh. So off to trial he went. It didn't take long for a jury of his peers to convict him.

So, about me. Client 1 was able to protect his identity. I wasn't. Many people in our fair town loved Mayor Marty. He had friends in many places, both high and low. Let's say it was fifty-fifty. About half of Lenore were lined up to pat me on the back, and the other half were out to slash my tires, or run me off the road, or whatever else they could do to get back at me for making these trumped-up charges against their pal Marty. I had been in a rather robust relationship with a Lenore High School biology teacher named Camille Hutton. To this day I find it so ironic considering my less than stellar history with high school biology. I still had no interest in growing plants or dissecting frogs, and she knew diddly-squat about the law, but we did have one thing in common. Neither one of us was looking for that walk-down-the-aisle ending. We were just two carnally expressive adults sharing a common interest. I know I was enjoying it. I found out when she ended our relationship that her father was besties with Mayor Marty. Daddy still had control over his little girl. Apparently, he called me a lowlife shyster or words to that effect. I guess blood is thicker than water. In addition to having my sex life abruptly interrupted, what Mayor Marty's supporters did to me that hurt more than anything else was they stopped using my expert legal services. There I go again, using that term "expert." The pain only lasted for a short time. Many of those good citizens who patted me on the back, thinking I must be a good, honest, and trustworthy lawyer, eventually became my clients. The reality was that I now had some enemies. Not only people who hated my guts over the Marty affair, but certain people who labeled me—unjustly so in my opinion—a troublemaker. Someone not to be trusted. Someone to be watched carefully. My grandfather was right, sometimes integrity comes at a high price.

So, who would replace Mayor Marty? According to municipal law, certain vacant positions could be filled by appointment. But not the lofty position of mayor. There had to be a by- election. Mayor Marty had run unopposed for his final two terms and the last one—as you now know—was interrupted. I think the entire town was shocked when two—yes two—candidates emerged. I know I was.

Candidate number one, and I'll list them in alphabetical order, was David Spencer. I didn't know a lot about him, but after meeting him for the first time, I liked him. I thought him to be honest, sincere, and hard-working—all the traits needed to run the enterprise that was the town of Lenore. He had served two terms on the Catholic school board. Not a lot of experience, but with a strong staff behind him, I thought he'd make a good mayor. Early on, at least in my head, I committed my vote to him. I even gave him my financial support, not exceeding the maximum allowed by law, of course.

Then there was the second candidate. Warren Winfield. I knew of him mostly by reputation. He had been a council member for three terms and a two-term member of the utilities board. To put it bluntly, he had been one of Mayor Marty's boys. Just to make sure I gave him a fair shake, due diligence as it's called, I attended a Vote for Warren rally. Read: fundraiser. He was a good-looking man. Like, Hollywood good-looking. Medium-brown hair, graying slightly around the temples to give him that experienced, but not old, look. He stood about six feet tall, maybe a smidge taller. Just tall enough, but not gangly looking. Clean-shaven, not that hip five o'clock stubble look. I wish I looked as good as he looked in a navy pin-striped suit. And the teeth. I'm certain that his dentist was now in a much higher tax bracket because of Candidate Winfield. And wouldn't you know it, he had the bluest eyes I've ever seen, like that shade of blue that you see on postcards showing the Mediterranean Sea, glistening in the sun.

How would I know his eyes were that blue? Candidate Winfield shook the hand of every attendee at his "rally" to make sure he could count on their vote and—just as importantly—their financial support.

He spent about thirty seconds of face time with me too. When he came over and introduced himself, I didn't give him my name. He probably already knew. His "people" pretty much had the name of everyone who was there, and I'm sure they connected me to the Mayor Marty affair. He should have thanked me. After all, if I hadn't upset Mayor Marty's apple cart, Warren wouldn't have had the opportunity to become mayor of Lenore. Who knows? Mayor Marty could have hung on for decades. You're welcome, Warren!

After he shook my hand, I had this uncontrollable urge to run into the men's room and scrub my hands with lye soap. And worse, after he moved on to re-enact the same introduction and handshake with the next voter slash donor, his scent lingered. Now don't get me wrong, I love it when you've been with a woman, whatever that means to you, and her scent is still in the air hours after she's gone. But in this case, it reminded me of how the smell of fried fish will hang around your house for days after being cooked. I don't know what it was, Hai Karate or Brut or some really nasty stuff. Maybe the women liked it, but it made my eyes water and my sinuses go crazy. I got out of there as quickly as I could. I needed to take a shower. And no, I did not leave a check in support of his candidacy.

The one thing that has always stuck in my head, and I don't know why, was Candidate Winfield's wife. They didn't seem to be a match, or even close to it. Now, I'm aware that many people thought that Sarah and I were a mismatch. And they were right. Mrs. Anne Winfield was not what you'd expect. She wasn't overweight or ugly or anything like that. Anne Winfield was plain. Just plain. When I first saw her hug the candidate, I thought maybe she was part of his campaign staff. Nope. The wife. The doting, "I'll be here for you no matter what, we're going to win this thing together" wife. Everything about her was nondescript. I can't remember the color of her hair or her dress. Nothing. I was looking for the trophy wife. Maybe someone like my ex, Sarah. Although the thought of her being Mrs. Warren Winfield made me laugh. It would be a constant battle as to who was the prettiest, Warren or Sarah. As hateful as this sounds, I thought Mrs. Winfield would be what the third-place finisher would get, the consolation prize. I knew for sure I was going to hell.

The campaign was over before it started. All of former Mayor Marty's folks were solidly behind Candidate Winfield. The women loved him. Even Peel. She thought he was a "doll." I told her that's not why you vote for someone, but I think she voted for him anyway.

My candidate, David Spencer, didn't stand a chance. It was a drubbing. Mayor-elect Winfield graciously accepted David's concession call. Looking back, that might have been the last gracious thing our new mayor ever did.

Out of all of this, something really good transpired. I had a new friend, David Spencer.

CHAPTER 3

DUE TO AN ODD QUIRK with the municipal laws, our new mayor not only got to finish out Mayor Marty's abbreviated term, he also got his own two-year term. I guess the lawmakers were concerned about the cost of mayoral elections back in 1931, when the law was enacted, well before the tax revenue was flowing like sangria at a Cinco de Mayo festival.

Mayor Winfield inherited a lot from Mayor Marty. A newly decorated office at town hall, for one. I was never granted an official audience with our new mayor, so I'm unable to offer a firsthand appraisal of his base of operations. I'm told there were three words often used to describe his office: *lavish*, *extravagant*, and *expensive*. Apparently, it had all the trappings that I had envisioned for my office before Peel burst that bubble and brought me back to reality. I was told that there was so much shiny brass one had to wear sunglasses when first entering the mayor's version of the Taj Mahal. Mayor Marty also bequeathed him a two-year-old Lincoln Navigator with a full-time driver slash bodyguard, Merle Atkinson. Ol' Merle had been transporting a Lenore mayor from place to place for many years. He may have been a great driver, but at five foot six, about 230 pounds, and turning sixty-three on his next birthday, a bodyguard he was not. No one knew for sure if Merle even carried a weapon he could use to defend the mayor's safety. And the reality was that in a town like Lenore, the mayor's well-being was seldom, if ever, at risk.

Maybe the best of Mayor Marty's estate, as I liked to call it, was that our new mayor inherited all his predecessor's loyalties on the town council. The new mayor would probably have agreed, although I never got the chance to ask him. There were eight council members. The mayor would only vote to break a tie, which hadn't happened even once during Mayor Marty's reign. And that was because five of the council members, and let's call them the Crew, had been in his pocket. Since he didn't have to campaign himself, Mayor Marty was able to campaign on behalf of his peeps. The five disciples owed their respective positions to him, and he made sure that not one of them ever forgot it. Especially when it came time to vote on any matters near and dear to the mayor's heart.

Now, Mayor Winfield enjoyed the same loyalty. Again, he didn't have to campaign after he completed Mayor Marty's term. He followed the same path. And, with his help, four council members were re-elected and the fifth was elected for the first time, replacing a retired member. And he ruled his crew with an iron hand. His endorsement of their future re-election campaigns was never guaranteed and they knew it. He met with them regularly, with the other three council members excluded. He gave the Crew information he didn't give to the Outsiders, as I started to call them. He didn't need their votes. He didn't care how they felt about issues. He simply ignored them. They would meet unofficially to vent their frustrations, knowing that their situation was a result of a numbers game and little could be done to change it. With tax revenues at an all-time high, the Crew voted themselves a nice raise. Rumor had it that one of the Outsiders refused to accept his newfound wealth. He had the additional funds sent to the animal shelter, where his wife served as a volunteer. Oh, I almost forgot: the council voted to give the mayor a 40 percent pay increase. It wasn't necessary for the mayor to vote or recuse himself from voting on his own raise. There was no tie.

Mayor Winfield added to his office's scope of control. He owned the local newspaper. I mean, he didn't own it in the conventional sense. The editor/owner, Clifford Parks, was the husband of his newest crew member, #5, Mrs. Dana Parks. Not that I cared. Honestly, I didn't have the time to follow local politics. Didn't have the temperament either. Up to this point I had been to one council meeting, to represent a client who had applied for a property separation so he could build his son a new home. His son was a wounded military veteran. The property committee had approved it. I attended the meeting to lobby on behalf of my client, if necessary. It wasn't. The vote was 8–0 in favor. But, to tell you the truth, I was bored out of my mind. I never went back, until I got a call from David Spencer. And that's how I found out about the raises.

I remember it was a Tuesday afternoon around four thirty. Peel put the call through.

"Hello, David. What's on your mind?"

Most of his calls were of a nonessential variety. More often than not he was calling to shoot the breeze.

"I thought I'd give my favorite attorney a call."

"I'd better be your only attorney."

And so, the banter began.

"What are you doing this evening?"

"David, are you asking me out . . . on a date?"

"Sort of."

"Does your beautiful wife know about your secret life?"

"Oh, sure. She encourages it. Gets me out of the house more often."

I realized that I was having far too great an influence on this fine, upstanding gentleman. He was starting to sound like me.

"So, what have you got in mind?"

"Are you busy . . . say around seven?"

"I'm afraid so, David. I have clients until six thirty. Then I'm having dinner with a beautiful woman at seven. Hopefully by nine I'll be making her fantasies about me come true."

"Liar."

Sometimes in our back-and-forth we have an unspoken contest: whoever laughs first loses. I lost this round.

"You're right. I look at my appointment book for this evening and I get snow blindness."

"Meet me at town hall at seven."

"Why?"

"Good stuff at the council meeting."

"Good maybe, but certainly not interesting. The last time I was there

I was bored out of my mind."

David pressed on. "Nothing boring about tonight, Counselor. Wouldn't you like to see our elected officials at work?"

"I hardly think what they do is work."

For me, looking forward to attending a council meeting was a lot like getting excited about a root canal. Watching grass grow held more excitement for me.

"For every thirty minutes you stay, I'll buy you a beer."

"Are you trying to bribe an officer of the court, David?"

"I am."

My response was immediate and totally expected.

"Agreed."

"You might want to get there before seven. No one gets in or out after that. Mayor's orders."

"We mustn't keep the mayor waiting."

CHAPTER 4

MY FIRST VISIT IN several years to the inner sanctum that was our council chambers was an eye-opener to say the least. David and I entered the hallowed hall shortly before seven. And on the dot, the doors closed. Obviously, Mayor Winfield ran a tight ship and I like that. My old friend Lenore Police Sergeant Len Stuckey stood guard to make sure no riffraff came or went after the appointed hour. We didn't speak or even acknowledge each other. Calling him my friend is probably a tad strong. We were acquainted, shall we say, professionally. He would never forgive me for making a fool out of him in court more than once. It was just too easy. How he made the rank of sergeant I will never know or understand. He was not the sharpest knife in the drawer. Not sure he was even in the drawer. Maybe the fact that he was the chief's brother-in-law had something to do with it.

Within a few minutes, the lights in the balcony magically dimmed and the lights over the long, curved council desk came on, illuminating the room as if a centuries-old religious ritual were about to take place.

Then the council members solemnly filed in procession-like. All eight of them; five for the Crew and three for the Outsiders. I'm not sure if there was a dress code for the members, but they were all suited up, including the newest member, Mrs. Dana Parks, who was wearing a dark blazer and white blouse. I have to admit that I was initially somewhat impressed. Apparently, some serious matters lay ahead and they were dressed accordingly. There was a high-backed, red velvet chair slightly elevated and strategically placed in the middle of the long desk. A light behind the chair made it glow. Facing the balcony, four members of the Crew sat to the left of the middle seat, with the fifth seated directly to the right. The Outsiders occupied the remaining seats to the right. After a pause of a few seconds that felt like ten minutes, Mayor Winfield made his grand entrance. All that was missing was the playing of "Hail to the Chief." He was wearing a navy-blue robe, trimmed in white braid, with the gold chain of office carefully placed around his neck. Later, I would refer to it as the hangman's noose. He didn't simply take a seat, he ascended to the throne. That most handsome of men looked so regal. I was waiting for the Crew to kiss the ring, but they had probably already done that in private.

I turned to David. "Do we bow or kneel or something? I'm new at this."

He ignored me.

Mayor Winfield called the meeting to order and off we went.

My unofficial count would be about thirty seats in the balcony where David and I positioned ourselves. Not the most comfortable chairs, but then again, I hoped I wouldn't be staying that long. Probably fifteen or twenty were occupied. I didn't recognize one other person. On the main floor, in front of the council desk and right behind the guest podium, were folding chairs for anyone who had direct business with the council that evening. Those seats looked even more uncomfortable than the ones we were seated in. I think maybe ten people had registered to address the council.

The reading of the last meeting's minutes by the clerk was first on the agenda. Yawn. There were several other items of business that followed, including an elderly lady who wanted her street renamed after her deceased cat. Now *that* I found interesting.

At precisely seven thirty, I turned to David and said, "Thirty minutes are up, pal. You owe me exactly one beer."

I was ignored again. David was really into this stuff.

At some point Lenore's chief of police was asked to introduce the two new additions to the force. One looked like he was about sixteen. The other could have been his younger brother. Guessing at their ages, I assumed that a postsecondary education wasn't a requirement to be a police recruit here in Lenore. The mayor preached on service, integrity, and commitment for at least twenty agonizing minutes, then they were sworn in.

I checked my watch. 8:01. It was now two beers.

David leaned over. "Now we come to the good part." Apparently, he had access to the evening's agenda. Good for him.

I looked to the heavens and mouthed, "Thank you!"

The recommendation for raises was read by the town's finance director.

Mayor Winfield pronounced from the throne that each member would be granted five minutes to express his or her position on the matter. Outsider 3, on the far-right side, objected at getting only five minutes.

This was the mayor's show. He brought the gavel down hard and loud. The limit would be five minutes.

I shouldn't have had that second beer before I left my condo. I had to pee like a racehorse.

Each of the Crew spoke for less than a minute. The Outsiders used the full five minutes to voice their displeasure. I was in pain.

The final result? You guessed it. The Crew: 5. The Outsiders: 3.

And it was over. Mayor Winfield adjourned the meeting.

I ran like an Olympic sprinter toward Sergeant Stuckey just as he opened the door. Thank goodness the men's room was only a few feet away in the lobby.

With a look of obvious relief on my face, and holding up four fingers, I walked up to David. "You owe me this many."

"Nope. Only three. The fourth half-hour was not completed."

"Spoken like a true politician."

He shook his head. "I am not a politician."

I nodded in mock agreement and replied, "Maybe not yet, but you will be. I saw that look on your face in there."

He just shook his head again. He knew I was right.

"I don't know about you, David, but I'm thirsty."

CHAPTER 5

IT HAD HAPPENED TO me before. Several times. At college, at law school, in court, and now in the sacred halls of government in Lenore. Mostly caused by beer, but often by coffee. When you have to pee—and I mean a DEFCON 5 emergency—you tend not to pay much attention to anything else that's going on. Like when a town council gives themselves a raise and the mayor is also on the receiving end of a boost in pay, his being astronomical. You can't multitask. Your only focus is on vacating your beleaguered bladder.

We left town hall and headed over to the Box Seat so I could collect my beer chips from David and, of course, to cash them in. There was no way I was going to down that many beers. I nursed just the one as David expressed his thoughts of the night's activities. He was vehemently opposed to the raises. I didn't have an opinion either way. David couldn't stop talking about it, virtually ruining the enjoyment of my earnings. He kept on and on. I just nodded.

It didn't register until the next morning, when I sat straight up in bed before my alarm normally interrupted my dream de nuit. Often my sleep, or at least the REM level, would be held hostage by one of three recurring dreams. Some nights I would be riding on the shoulders of my Lenore High School teammates after I had scored the winning touchdown to claim the state championship. That never happened. And there had been no chance of that ever happening, certainly not with the talent we had on that team, or the lack thereof. In the second dream I was being sworn in as the chief justice of the Supreme Court. Not an ounce of reality there. But it was the third one that caused most of my head scratching. I could never figure out why I would be dreaming about frolicking in a hot tub or on the beach with Mallory McCutcheon. I hoped that she had been long forgotten, but nope, she appeared at least a couple of times a week to confuse and distract me. Often in various stages of undress. For whatever reason, this morning I simply sat straight up in bed, wide awake, realizing that the good citizens of Lenore, myself being one, had just been screwed by our elected officials.

Over coffee and an English muffin at my kitchen table, I came up with a plan. It was simple but brilliant, in my humble opinion.

Initially I didn't have much against Mayor Winfield other than I just didn't like him. And of course, there was the business of him being one of Mayor Marty's boys. I guess that alone gave me reason not to like this guy. But now it was beyond dislike. And added to that, I didn't trust him. I wanted to put a label on him and his crew. Crooks, Scumbags, Liars. I'd think of something, not that they weren't all those things.

My genius plan was to write a letter to Clifford Parks, the editor/

owner of our fine, upstanding twice-weekly newspaper: the *Lenore Gazette*, the Voice of Greater Lenore. I'm guessing that Lesser Lenore didn't qualify to have a voice.

Some of my highest grades in law school were achieved in legal writing. Now, don't get the idea that I was on the Dean's Honor List. I might have been on a list or two, but it wasn't that one. I knew how to write a letter, and I wanted this letter to the editor to be one of my best. I can safely testify that it was. I wrote about how hardworking citizens had to sacrifice and save just to stay one step ahead of financial disaster. That one made me smile. I was off to a good start. A car salesman would have to work longer hours to sell more cars to get a raise. An hourly paid worker would have to endure hours and hours of overtime, away from his family, to give himself a raise of this magnitude. I was on a roll. But our elected officials, now that's a different story altogether. By simply saying "aye" in a council meeting, they gave themselves a raise that was not only undeserved, but unjustified and downright inappropriate. Pretty good, huh? Then I took aim at the mayor. I pointed out that at no time in our recent history had any civil servant, in any way connected to Lenore, been a party to such an egregious raise in pay. An honest office-holder with a backbone would have declined the increase in the interests of the good citizens of Lenore. But not our mayor. Yep, I said that. I continued by praising the three Outsiders; they were the only ones in council who had scruples. And yes, I said that too. If the council had a collective conscience, they would reconsider the raises and vote them down. But I doubted that would happen. *Good citizens of Lenore, bend over and grab your ankles. Yep, you lose again. To the mayor and members of council, see you at the polls next year.*

Peel printed it out on office letterhead, addressed an envelope, and sealed it. Along with the appropriate postage, away it went. I even emailed a copy to David. I knew I'd get a response.

"You mailed it?"

"Peel did."

"You're my hero. Wanna have sex?" He laughed.

I was speechless. No question about it, I was having a bad influence on David. Honestly, I was enjoying this heretofore hidden side of my friend.

There was one fly in the ointment regarding my letter to the editor. It didn't get printed. David had pointed out that the editor/owner of our prestigious newspaper, Mr. Clifford Parks, was in bed with the mayor. Not literally. More by marital proxy. So I knew that the editor's wife, Mrs. Dana Parks, was the newest member of the Crew. I have no idea why I thought my letter would get printed. As Homer Simpson has said on many occasions, "Doh!"

The sensible thing to do would have been to throw my hands in the air and walk away. Nope. Couldn't do that. So I emailed a copy to the editor. Same result. Then I called him several times, leaving messages, without ever getting a call back.

He did write and print an op-ed praising the mayor and the council for the great work they were doing. The raises weren't mentioned.

I sent a final email. I told him that I knew his wife was one of the mayor's crew and that by extension so was he. The only voice that would be heard via the *Gazette* would be that of the mayor. No one else. I told him I was a citizen of Lenore, a taxpayer, and I wasn't going anywhere.

I finished by saying that he hadn't heard the last of me. Legally not a threat, but I wanted him to think it was.

The readers of the *Lenore Gazette* never got the opportunity to read my letter. I'd bet the farm that the mayor did—every word and every email. It wasn't the "shot heard round the world," but it was a shot across the bow of Mayor Winfield. I could be many things in the mayor's eyes. Ignored wasn't going to be one of them.

I could no longer sit on the sidelines. I decided to take up a new hobby. I was going to be the biggest boil on Mayor Winfield's butt, left or right cheek, it didn't matter. A boil so big that even Dr. Pimple Popper would gasp. And every time he sat down he would think of me.

CHAPTER 6

MY FIRST DUTY, ON my campaign to be a giant growth on the mayor's behind, was to show up at each and every council meeting. I called it "benign harassment." I told David about my tactical approach and got a thumbs-up. He would accompany me every chance he could, but his wife was expecting baby number four, so his availability on Tuesday nights would be hit and miss. I was OK with that. Daddy duties took precedence over stalking the mayor of Lenore.

On a sidenote, the editor/owner of the *Lenore Gazette* made a significant error twice a week: he put his picture on the upper left-hand corner of the editorial page. On my first night flying solo at the council meeting I arrived a little early in order to hit the head before the proceedings got underway. Although I hadn't consumed any beer that evening, just in case, I didn't want to punish my bladder again. Sure enough, as I'm coming out of the men's room, guess who's going in? Yep, the editor/owner of the *Lenore Gazette*, Mr. Clifford Parks, and I recognized him. They must have airbrushed his photo. This was not a handsome man. So I hung around the lobby, waiting for him to come back out. I walked up to him with my arm extended, addressing him by name. He smiled and shook my hand. Apparently, he didn't know who I was. His hand was damp. I hoped it was because he had just washed it, as opposed to the other explanation.

"Hi, I'm Brett Simmons. Why didn't you print my letter? Why don't you answer my emails? Why don't you return phone calls?"

He looked like he had run into a mass murderer in a dark alley and was about to become my next victim. I'm bigger and stronger than him, so I held on to his hand firmly. He tried to get away, but I wouldn't let him. I could see panic in his eyes. Obviously, he was a lover, not a fighter. Finally, I released his hand and he scurried off like a roach when someone turns the light on.

I can't be certain if what happened next was caused by my short, one-sided conversation with the editor/owner or my unpublished letter. Probably both.

I had just taken my seat in the balcony and was adjusting the volume on my little portable recorder, which I had purchased for this very occasion, when I looked up to see my old friend Sgt. Len Stuckey. He was motioning me with his right index finger to leave my seat and follow him.

"Please come with me, Mr. Simmons."

And of course, I responded with my usual sarcasm.

"Am I under arrest, Sergeant?"

He didn't answer.

I went with him out of the council chambers, back into the lobby. Waiting for us was the chief of police, Cal Pryor, accompanied by one of those boy-men I had witnessed being sworn in the previous week. They were an ominous-looking pair. I would hate to be a fleeing criminal with these three fine representatives of our police force in hot pursuit: a chief who couldn't catch an old lady shoplifting, a sergeant with the IQ of a speed bump, and a rookie cop with a bad case of adolescent acne.

"What can I do for you, Chief?"

"Mr. Simmons, are you familiar with Lenore Bylaw 83dash9dash41?"

"You got me on that one, Chief. I didn't know that was going to be on the exam. I would have studied harder. Wait, I'm already a lawyer, I should know the answer. I'm embarrassed."

He wasn't amused.

"In a nutshell, Mr. Simmons, Bylaw 83dash9dash41 gives the mayor the authority to refuse entry to council meetings of anyone he chooses."

I knew right away where this was going.

"And let me guess: It's my lucky day. He chose me."

Again, my humor totally escaped him.

"Mr. Simmons, you can look it up if you wish."

"Now, why would I want to do that? I believe you. You're the chief of police, for gosh sakes."

"And you're going to have to surrender your cell phone, Mr. Simmons."

I knew immediately that wasn't going to happen.

"Excuse me?"

"Your cell phone, Mr. Simmons. We are going to confiscate it. You may have taken pictures or made audio recordings inside the council chambers."

"This is where I take over, Chief Pryor. Apparently, I can be refused entry to the council meeting. I won't argue that one. But, from the by-law designation number, it was first enacted in 1983. And if memory serves, Chief, cell phones weren't on the market. So, for you to get my cell phone, you'll need a court order. You know, a subpoena. A search warrant. Something with a judge's signature on it. And anyway, the meeting hasn't even started yet. What was I supposed to record, the sound of spectators taking their seats?"

He still had his hand out, thinking I was going to hand it over.

"A court order, Chief. Do you have one? If you physically try to take it from me, I will make sure that after I sue you, the mayor, and the town of Lenore, you'll have trouble getting a job checking parking meters in Hooterville."

He put his hand down.

"Now, Chief, if you'll excuse me, I will leave the premises and allow you to get on with crime fighting and keeping Lenore a safe place to live. Have a nice evening, gentlemen."

I had only taken a few steps when I remembered my newly purchased portable audio recorder, in which I had invested $19.95 plus tax. It was going to be a better investment than I had initially thought. I turned back around and handed it to the chief.

"I got some good stuff on this handy-dandy device. I'll share a little secret with you. I hid the little cassette in my anal cavity. The first time, it was a tight squeeze and a little uncomfortable, but now it slips right in there, lickety-split. Care to check, Chief?"

It was like they were frozen in time, jaws wide open. They had no idea how to respond.

"Evening, gentlemen."

I walked out and headed for my car.

As soon as I got in the Duster, I called David on my cell and gave him the rundown of my interesting night. He laughed, especially at the cassette story.

"Seems like you've become public enemy number one," David said after I finished.

"I hope so. I won the trifecta. I got to meet the editor/owner of the newspaper, scared the chief of police into thinking he might have to shine a flashlight up my butt, and, most importantly, I got the mayor's attention. Ain't we havin' fun now?"

CHAPTER 7

WHEN I FIRST MET David Spencer, he was, in a word, stiff. But he loosened up as our friendship grew stronger. No question about it, I was a bad influence on him. Sometimes, when we were together without a chaperone, we would revert to our college days, or at least I would. I can't confirm nor deny if beer was involved. I'll let you decide. We laughed and joked around, making fun of everyone and everything, including ourselves. And of course our favorite targets were the elected officials of our beloved town of Lenore.

We could be serious should the situation warrant. As I recall, I failed to hide my displeasure at his decision not to enter the upcoming municipal election as a candidate. If not for the position of mayor, at least he could try to unseat one of the Crew. Reluctantly, I embraced his decision. His wife had just delivered baby number four to the Spencer household, and things were probably a little hectic over there.

At lunch one day he made the unofficial announcement: "I've been talking to Julie."

"Your wife? You talk to your wife?"

He ignored my comment and continued: "I have received her blessing to enter the next municipal election as a candidate."

I put my fork down and pointed at him. "She's stringing you along, old buddy. With current elections in two weeks, that puts it more than two years away. She's going to get pregnant again, and Spencer baby number five will preempt your candidacy. She's a good Catholic girl."

"Nope. I'm going to have some plumbing work done on the boys."

I gave him my phony shocked look. "Your sons? Your beautiful sons, who, thankfully, get their looks from their mother?"

In return, I got the look of disgust.

"No, dirtbag. The ones between my legs."

"Oh, those boys. As in the Big V?"

"Yep," David said, almost proudly.

"Ouch! Is it true that after a guy gets the snip-snip his voice gets higher?"

"Where did you get that from?" David asked in disbelief.

"Duh . . . the internet. So it has to be true."

Although he knew I was jerking his chain, he gave me that "you're an idiot" look.

"No. I will still be a baritone and the same stud muffin I have always been."

I made a scrunchy face and said, "Sorry, David, I just threw up in my mouth."

I felt a little relief and a lot of pride knowing that at some point in the future my friend would become a politician, again. He was defeated in his last attempt, and I had always hoped the memory of that experience wouldn't stop him from taking another go in the political arena.

Unfortunately, this election turned out as predicted. I felt like I was watching the movie *Groundhog Day* and I was whoever Bill Murray played. Mayor Winfield ran unopposed. The score between the hometown Crew and the visiting Outsiders: 5 to 3 in favor of the Crew. Another two years of the same old, same old.

Since I was persona non grata at the weekly council meetings, I had to think of other ways to maintain my status as the official boil on the butt of our beloved mayor. I thought about becoming a blogger. With my distinct lack of expertise in the area of computers, websites, and all the technology, I decided to leave that to someone who knew what they were doing.

Speaking of computers, I did know how to use one. I was not totally technologically illiterate, but I had to give in and recognize the need to enter into a service contract with an independent IT specialist to take care of my hardware and software. And, like my marriage to Sarah, this relationship was short-lived as well. One day, I went to lunch at the Chelsea and saw my guy—the one who had access to anything and everything on my office and personal computers—breaking bread with a member of none other than the Crew. My second ugly divorce. I had to pay him alimony to cover the remaining months of the service agreement. I should have got a prenup. Eventually I found the right guy, and after a lengthy interview process, I discovered that he held similar views to my own regarding our local government. A match made in heaven.

I decided to continue with my campaign of civil disobedience. At random intervals I would write letters to the editor, sending them by snail mail and email, knowing of course they would never get published. But it did give me great satisfaction knowing I had a direct channel to the mayor since I was convinced he read every one of them, and those letters were serving as a reminder to King Warren that what had started out as a pimple on his gluteus maximus was not going away.

CHAPTER 8

THERE'S AN OLD SAYING, "He couldn't see the forest for the trees." The "he" in this case would be me. It was right in front of me all the time, hiding in plain sight. The letter writing was having little effect, I thought. It had become old hat and I needed a new tactic. Since I couldn't go to the council meetings, I could either read the *Gazette* or team up with someone who could attend. The *Gazette* would give me the dessert. I needed the meat and potatoes. Who else but one of the Outsiders? Why hadn't I thought of that before?

I had my choice of three. The Outsider to the far right of center—not politically speaking, but on the seating chart—was just too over-the-top for me. Denny Moffett was a veteran of local politics. He had a reputation for being very intense with a short fuse. I saw him as a potential loose cannon, although I did respect his opinions, particularly those he held about our mayor and his crew. And he wore a bow tie. He reminded me of my high school biology teacher. He always wore a bow tie. I eliminated him immediately.

The second choice was Ted Burwell, a retired schoolteacher. He seemed like a nice guy, but there was a calmness about him that set off an alarm for me. When it came time to rock the boat Ted would probably still be standing on the dock, like a spectator. Nope, not him.

Outsider #3 was my last hope. I needed someone whose temperament stood somewhere between the fiery Bow Tie Denny and the tranquil Ted Burwell. Brad Perryman was an accountant; a sole proprietor, an entrepreneur like me, so I decided to approach him. He returned my email the same day. A good sign. I had asked him if he would meet me for coffee sometime to discuss matters of mutual interest regarding Lenore and its future. He replied that he didn't drink coffee, but perhaps we could get together for a beer. And what do you think my reply was? How about today? We met a little after five thirty at the Marriott. Turns out he knew my grandfather. Small world.

After a few get-acquainted minutes, we got down to serious discussion. He remembered me from the Mayor Marty incident. I told him about my friendship with David Spencer. He said that he had voted for David in the election that, unfortunately, saw Warren Winfield come out victorious. I shared my story about Lenore Bylaw 83dash9dash41 and not being able to attend council meetings. He just smiled and nodded his head.

Driving home later, I made up my mind that Mr. Brad Perryman was my guy. I called David to tell him.

"So you found an ally, Counselor?"

"I did. He hasn't said yes, but I'm sure he will join us on our crusade.

Let's say he's not a fan of our mayor and his crew."

I guess I got David's attention.

"And then there were three. What are we going to call ourselves, Brett?"

I had already been thinking about a name. "Maybe a little corny, but how about the A Team? *A* for *allies.*"

"I like it."

It took little convincing to persuade Brad to join our merry band of outlaws. Spiritually he was one of us before he or anyone else knew it. He saw the mayor in the same light as David and I did. He was frustrated that he couldn't fairly and properly represent his ward. His voters really had no voice at council because of the mayor's exclusion of him and the other Outsiders. He was on one barely visible committee: Public Works. He had been pushing for the creation of an Ethics Committee, with zero success. He needed to have his hands untied, and he saw our little group as a way to get that done. He loved Lenore as Brad and I did. I knew he would be a perfect fit.

It took one more phone call for Brad to consent to join us. We would meet occasionally to discuss events at town hall and in council and to plot our strategies.

We needed to advertise, but not in the normal sense. I mean, the *Gazette* probably would have turned us down. I could never imagine owner/editor Parks running a story on the good works of the A Team. Anyway, we didn't need the general public to know who we were and what we were doing, just the mayor and his crew. After some research we discovered that the editor/owner of the *Gazette* and his bride, Crew Member

#5, had lunch at the Chelsea every Wednesday at twelve thirty, and they always sat at the same table. This particular hump day the A Team assembled at the adjoining table at about twelve fifteen. We put twenty dollars each in a pool. I said they would leave as soon as they saw us. Brad said they would still have lunch at their usual table, but most uncomfortably. David, the eternal optimist, said they would be nonplussed. They would simply ignore the A Team and enjoy their lunch. With sixty bucks at stake, I began to hum Carly Simon's "Anticipation." We had already ordered and were in the middle of nibbling our salads, without a leaf of kale to be found, as the happy couple walked in. When they spotted us they stopped dead in their tracks. Immediately #5 went to the front desk and demanded another table. She was obviously in control. The sixty bucks went unclaimed.

After they were seated, Brad waved. It was ignored. So he got up and went over to speak to the lady in charge, one council member to another. His attempt at being sociable was not well received. Our presence probably drove them to eat much more quickly than normal. After she motioned to the waiter for the check, I got up and went over to their table with a simple question of how one went about getting an annual subscription to the *Gazette*, not that I would ever sign up. He didn't answer. If her glare had been ice, I'd be frozen solid. She said, "Sir, just call the paper." I thanked her and returned to my seat. They stormed out, with #5 in the lead and the editor/owner meekly taking up the rear.

For some reason I thought about the First Lady of Lenore. If Mrs. Winfield was plainly forgettable, #5 was the opposite. When I first saw her, as she accompanied the other council members as they solemnly walked into that council meeting, I had recognized that Dana Parks was very attractive. I mean, a looker. She stood at least three inches taller than the love of her life. Her hair was a soft brown with lighter brown highlights, falling neatly just above her shoulders. Her lipstick was a soft red. Someone had taught Mrs. Parks the fine art of what to wear and when to wear it. And more importantly, what not to wear. It would seem that her choice of clothing was always well thought out. This day, she was sporting a navy blazer with medium-gray slacks. A string of pearls lay over the collar of her pale-blue silk blouse. Classy. I have no idea what he was wearing. I paid little if any attention to him, other than my obviously fake question about a subscription. Not a word was spoken as the A Team watched her leave. She left an impression.

Over the next few months we made several more strategic appearances. For some unknown reason, the Law Society of Dunham County chose Mayor Warren Winfield as its Man of the Year. I voted for the Lenore Fire Chief. He was retiring after thirty years of service. A much more deserving choice in my mind. I was able to purchase two additional tickets to the event, and on the attendee list, David and Brad were placed under my name as my guests. I'm sure the mayor was made aware of our presence, which, in fact, was all we were trying to do.

The second full term of Mayor Winfield was remarkable in its lack of excitement. Not much of anything notable happened. Through legal, closed-bid processes, he privatized the collection of solid waste, the Water Department, and the management of the municipal swimming pool. I had to wonder how much additional, unreported cash it took to secure a winning bid. Wink, wink. Business as usual in the Winfield administration. Two more townhouse developments were completed, totaling

184 units. One day, almost hidden on the back page of the *Gazette*, was the announcement, among other real estate transactions, that an option had been taken out on a tract of land on Route 81, just inside the town limits. No details were given, and I paid little attention to it.

Little did I know that tract of land would become forever connected with those two previously mentioned words of legalese.

CHAPTER 9

TO SAY THAT THE mayor's second full term was relatively uneventful didn't mean that it was without incident. It was about nine months before the next municipal election. The A Team was meeting at Brad's place to discuss campaign strategies. We couldn't meet at my place due to a lack of visitor parking. David's house was overrun with ankle biters, four below the age of eight. Brad and his wife, Sylvia, were empty nesters, so their place was perfect. Had I known, I would have made a pit stop on the way over, but I didn't find out until I got there: Brad was out of beer. Normally panic would have ensued, but we kept our heads, and for the next couple of hours we sipped on Sylvia's iced tea. Lucky for me, that was the sole refreshment for the evening.

The main topic was David's campaign. Where was he going to run? His own ward, the area in which he lived, or one of the at-large seats on the council, of which there were two? It was decided that he should stay closer to home. It was ultimately David's call. The incumbent was, of course, a member of the Crew. We all agreed he was vulnerable. He had won Ward 4 in the previous election but only by a small margin, something like seventy-four votes. His opponent at the time was not able to run in this upcoming election due to health issues. Enter David. We would be there to support him in any way we could.

We wrapped things up around nine thirty. David took a left on Route 81. I should have done the same, but the mid-April evening was downright beautiful and my girl, the Duster, was in need of a good run, so I turned right, heading in the direction of King City. I sang Chuck Berry's "Maybelline" as I took her up to seventy-five miles per hour. About fifteen miles out of K.C. I turned around in the conservation area parking lot and headed back to Lenore.

I had no more than passed the Welcome to Lenore sign when in my rearview appeared the flashing blue lights. The sound of the siren hit my ears a few seconds later. My immediate reaction was to check the speedometer. I was doing exactly forty-five miles per hour, which was the designated maximum speed. I pulled over to the curb, the police car pulling in behind.

I'm not sure if this officer knew traffic stop protocol, especially after 10:00 p.m. on a dark and deserted stretch of Route 81. He walked right up to the driver's-side door and tapped on the window, which I obediently rolled down.

The chief of police had been on a recruiting binge again. This young man was obviously new and probably unsure of himself.

"Good evening, Officer."

"Driver's license, registration, and proof of insurance, sir."

Now you may have noticed that I have a habit of opening my mouth several seconds before my brain has kicked in. And this was one of those times.

As I handed him my documents I said, "Son, do your parents know you're out this late?" I thought it was funny at the time. He did not.

He walked back to his vehicle with the purpose of running me through the system. I'm convinced that he had been tipped off as to my identity and on which side of the road, politically speaking, I was parked.

After several minutes, he came back.

Again, I couldn't help myself. "If you need an alibi when you get home, I'll swear you spent the whole evening with me."

I got no reaction. Zero.

"Get out of the car, sir. I'm going to administer a field sobriety test."

And this is when I realized that this had been one of the rare instances where running out of beer was a good thing.

Now I don't want you to get the idea that I routinely drove around Lenore in an inebriated state. I did not. Maybe a little buzz going on, but never, ever legally drunk. My grandfather liked a cold beer, maybe more than one. I remember him telling me, "It's not worth it, Brett. Not worth it. Get a cab, call a friend, do something, but if you're the least bit likely to get a DUI attached to your name, leave the car keys in your pocket." He never told me, and I never asked, but I had this sense that he was speaking from experience.

So I obeyed the youngster's command and got out of the car, knowing I had nothing to be concerned about.

We were standing between his vehicle and mine when he asked me the all-important police question heard around the world on a nightly basis, "Have you been drinking tonight, sir?"

"If a pitcher of Red Rose Iced Tea with lemon and a pinch of stevia is considered drinking, then I guess I have." Now why did I say that?

Just then the sensible lawyer in me overtook the wise-cracking one.

"Do you understand that according to laws regarding traffic stops, Officer, I can refuse the normal sobriety tests, such as following your finger side to side without moving my head, or counting backwards from a hundred, or standing on one leg without falling over? I can request a breathalyzer test, which I hereby do."

He looked overwhelmed. He had probably heard about this at the police academy, but this was the first time it had ever happened to him in the line of duty.

"Do you have a breathalyzer machine in your squad car, Officer?"

"Stay right where you are, sir. Don't move." And with that, he got back in his vehicle and I saw him talking on the two-way radio.

He sat there for quite some time, until I heard the siren coming up behind me. I turned my head slightly to see more flashing blue lights. I'm not sure why the siren and the blue lights. I wasn't resisting arrest and I wasn't a suspect in a major drug ring. A slight overkill, but it must have been a quiet night with little criminal activity in Lenore. Or maybe an attempt at intimidation. The second police car made a U-turn right there in the middle of Route 81 and pulled up behind the other car. It looked like we had ourselves a convoy.

And you'll never guess who stepped out of the recently arrived squad car. Of course, my old friend Sgt. Len Stuckey. And that answered my question about the siren and the blue lights.

"Good evening, Sergeant. Working late I see. I've just been having a conversation with your young compadre here about laws regarding traffic stops. Do you want to tell him or should I?"

Apparently, the sergeant was in no mood to play, so I responded to my own question.

"I'm an attorney, son. A lawyer. An officer of the court," I said, trying to be as clear as possible.

He looked at Sergeant Stuckey, not knowing how to respond.

"Alright, Mr. Simmons, what's this all about? Are you refusing to take a sobriety test?"

"Oh no, not at all. It's just that the law says I get to choose the method. And I choose breathalyzer, Sergeant," I replied with a grin.

He walked back to his car and returned with a box that looked like it had never been opened. He fumbled getting the machine out of its place of safekeeping.

"Do you know how to use one of those things, Sergeant? I can help you if you like. Be careful. Those devices have been known to injure untrained operators."

I guess I was the only one present who failed to see the seriousness in the situation.

Finally, he was ready to administer the test.

"Now, Mr. Simmons, blow as hard as you can into the tube until I tell you to stop."

I complied.

When he told me to stop, both he and his junior partner looked at the meter. There appeared to be some kind of confusion within the ranks of the local constabulary.

"We're going to have to do this again, Mr. Simmons."

"Nope. I'm guessing that the meter read zero point zero zero parts per thousand, which I could have told you before you went to all this trouble. Legally drunk is point oh eight parts per thousand. And guess what? According to the previously mentioned laws, you only get one shot at it, Sergeant. And you just had yours. I'm sorry you had to drive all the way out here for nothing. So now that you've completed your little science project, I'll be on my way."

With that, the sergeant removed his nightstick from its holster. Now, most modern police forces issue those new collapsible batons that click when they open. But not here in Lenore. Ol' Sergeant Stuckey, an old-schooler, had one of those black jobs, from bygone years, that would hang down the outside of his right leg, and if he ever had to run, which probably hadn't happened lately, that nightstick would beat the daylights out of his leg. Right about this time he recognized his opportunity. He probably remembered how I had thoroughly embarrassed him in court. He calmly walked over to my car and, with said nightstick, broke the passenger-side taillight assembly of my beloved '72 Plymouth Duster.

Glass shards flew in all directions.

"Mr. Simmons, it seems you have a broken taillight."

I won't hazard a guess as to what kind of reaction he was expecting, but I am sure he was surprised by the one he got. Despite the furor quickly rising inside me and the urge to take the nightstick from the sergeant and shove it so deep into one of his body cavities it would require surgery to have it removed, I responded calmly. Thinking back, I know I could have taken both of them. A knee to the groin and a jab to his ample midsection would have disabled the sergeant. Probably yelling "boo" to his protégé would have sent him running home to Mommy. Problem with that is they could have called in backup, as in the entire Lenore police force. I was the Lone Ranger with no Tonto in sight. And my evening would have ended in one of the two holding cells back at police HQ. Discretion was the better part of valor.

"You are absolutely right, Sergeant. Thank you so much for pointing that out to me. I shouldn't be driving an unsafe vehicle. I'll get that fixed right away."

He then walked to the front of the Duster, opened the driver's-side door, took the keys out of the ignition, and promptly threw them over the car, into the long grass on the other side of the water-filled ditch, which was probably snake infested.

"What a beautiful night, Mr. Simmons. Perfect for a long walk."

He and his mini-me got into their respective vehicles and drove off, leaving me alone on Route 81 with zero bars showing on my cell phone and standing beside my precious '72 Plymouth Duster, now injured, and without any way to start her up and limp home.

* * *

I did not walk home that evening. The marines would have been proud of me. I adapted. By dragging my heel across the gravel shoulder of the road, next to the broken glass, I made a fairly deep groove so I could easily find the location in the daylight, which I did the next morning, recovering my keys. The Boy Scouts would have been proud of me. I was prepared. I got back in the Duster, reached under the floor mat, and retrieved my extra set. The only hiking I did that night was from my designated place in the underground parking garage to the elevator.

And I wasn't going to let Sergeant Stuckey get by with desecrating my classic beauty. Nope. The drive that night from the scene of the defilement to the condo gave me time to plan my revenge. I took the Duster into the shop, Bobby's Auto Body and Restoration. Bobby had found her originally, restored her, and sold her to me. I think he loved her as much as I did. He was more than dismayed to see the damage inflicted on her by Sergeant Stuckey. Not only is it challenging to find a taillight assembly for a '72 Plymouth Duster, but once you find one, it's very expensive. I mean, sticker-shock expensive. I could have involved my insurance company, but how was I supposed to answer the question "Did you fill out a police report?" Hmmm.

Bobby was unable to give me an ETA on the repair, so he loaned me a rather inconspicuous, gray, eight-year-old Honda Accord, which fit into my plan rather nicely.

* * *

Boys will be boys. Yep, we will. I remember Stevie Brant, Frankie Smithson, and me being creative pranksters. Old Man Thorold was a most deserving target. He was mean-spirited and didn't like anyone, particularly kids. And we didn't like him. One hot summer's evening, we took a burlap bag, filled it with fresh cow manure, placed it on his front doorstep, poured lighter fluid on it, set it on fire, then rang the doorbell and ran like hell. From behind a tree we could see Old Man Thorold stomping on the bag trying to put out the fire, with bovine excrement flying all over the porch and all over him.

I wasn't about to stoop to the level of teenage pranksters. I was a lawyer, a mature professional. Uh-huh.

* * *

It was the next Tuesday evening. I set out from the condo in the gray Honda, dressed in my black jogging suit, black running shoes, and black driving gloves. I looked like a ninja. The only things missing were eye black, which I would have applied to my face if I'd had any, and a set of nunchucks. I parked the Honda on the street adjacent to the rear of the municipal offices. From my tactical vantage point I was able to see Sergeant Stuckey arriving. I guessed, looking at the rust above the wheel wells and the broken mirror on the passenger side, that some serious mileage had accumulated on his Dodge Caravan. He brought it to rest, with brakes squeaking, at the far end of the parking lot, under a maple tree. The front of the minivan was almost in darkness. Perfect.

He exited his vehicle at exactly 6:15 p.m. That gave me about forty-five minutes to wait. I was ready. The mission was underway. Too late to abort.

I don't do the waiting thing very well. At the doctor's office, the dentist, the optometrist, I get restless and fidgety. This night was no different.

I decided to focus on the mayor, his cohorts, and what new schemes they were inflicting on the good citizens of Lenore, inside the council chambers. Believe it or not, I couldn't concentrate. That never happens. Never. My thoughts were flying all over the place. *What if I get caught?* A big fine, probably some jail time. I doubt I would have gotten disbarred, but more than likely I'd have been suspended from practicing law. I could hear my grandfather saying, "Go for it." Then my grandmother took over: "Remember the gospel, Brett. 'Vengeance is mine sayeth the Lord.'" What sustained me was the mental picture of Sergeant Stuckey inflicting such pain on my baby. That renewed my resolve.

Finally, at 7:05, knowing that the council meeting had started and that Sergeant Stuckey was squarely at his post, I got out of the Honda. I walked slowly to the parking lot and headed for the Dodge Caravan, holding a tire iron firmly in my hand. Wrapped around my weapon of choice was an old, oil-stained towel I got from Bobby's. The towel would mute the sound of breaking glass.

Luckily, a light rain had started to fall and the parking lot was devoid of human activity except for the stealthy movements of the Ninja Warrior.

The headlight on the driver's side took two blows from the tire iron before succumbing. The one on the passenger's side was felled by the first strike. The rag muffled the noise. I calmly walked back to the Honda satisfied that my mission had been a success.

I had heard of the theory that a criminal will often return to the scene of the crime. Yep. I mean, I hadn't considered what I was doing a criminal act, but yes, I got out of the Honda and went back to the minivan and let the air out of both front tires. Looking at the condition of the tires, I knew I had barely beaten Father Time to the job.

Returning to the Honda a second time and ready to make my escape, I looked down at the passenger seat and staring back at me was a bottle of Gatorade, about half full. Then I heard this strange voice in my head. It was the sensei. "Your mission is not yet complete, Grasshopper." Yep, I took the remainder of the Gatorade and poured it into the gas tank of that Dodge Caravan.

Retribution was sweet. As I drove away I said out loud, "Sergeant Stuckey, payback is hell."

Mission accomplished. Well done, Ninja Warrior. Well done.

CHAPTER 10

THE NEXT EDITION OF the *Gazette* carried a story about some vandalism at the municipal offices involving the private vehicle of one of Lenore's finest. I always read the *Gazette* sitting on my personal throne, which paled in comparison to the mayor's. Mine was made of porcelain. An appropriate place, I thought, to do some casual, forgettable reading.

I purchased the Honda from Bobby. I sublet a second space in the underground parking garage from Mrs. Hanley, in 604. At eighty-four, she couldn't drive anymore. More accurately, her license was taken away after a minor fender bender at a quiet intersection one Sunday morning. I had decided to drive the Duster on special occasions, never at night out on Route 81.

David had filed his papers to be a candidate in the upcoming municipal elections. He had asked me to be his campaign manager. I gracefully declined. It was well known in some circles that we were friends. I just didn't want it in writing. His next-door neighbor accepted the unpaid position. In reality, David did most of the legwork himself. Of course,

Brad had his own campaign to run, with Sylvia listed as his manager. I helped both campaigns wherever and whenever I could. Typically, the first few months were calm. The storm would blow in during the last month or so prior to Election Day.

Then something unexpected happened. The mayor, in his infinite wisdom, decided that the final few minutes of each council meeting would be taken up for a Q&A session. Fifteen minutes to be precise. A great PR move right before an election. Like a town hall meeting, anyone could ask pretty much anything of the mayor, the Crew, or the Outsiders. The term *anyone* meant anyone who was in attendance and had not been excommunicated under Lenore Bylaw 83dash9dash41.

Apathy ruled the day. It seems this opportunity to express one's views to our elected officials didn't interest many takers. In fact, it only attracted one: Wendy Tolliver. She was the HOA president of Tanglewood Estates. Read: townhouses. Week after week she came armed with a list of problems. The truck collecting trash for recycling had failed to pick up the bag left out by one of her owners, as she called them. Several of her owners were complaining about woodpeckers damaging privacy fences. A drainage ditch overflowed every time it rained. The standard response was, "We'll look into it, Mrs. Tolliver."

I asked Brad, who was present and accounted for each week, why the mayor allowed it to continue. You know, the infamous Lenore Bylaw. He could have put her on the sidelines, next to me. This may have been the only time that the mayor and all eight council members, the Crew and the Outsiders, as one voice, agreed on anything; that Wendy Tolliver was not just eccentric, she was crazy. Certifiable. Her ramblings became entertainment at the end of the council meetings.

But Wacko Wendy was not satisfied with her weekly appearance at the municipal offices. Nope. On the final day for citizens to file documents with the election commission, WW did just that. She would run for mayor. She would become a thorn in the side of Mayor Warren Winfield, which of course was several rungs lower in prestige to the position of boil on the butt of His Majesty.

And her place of residence in Tanglewood Estates was in Ward 4, David's bailiwick. We met with her several times during the campaign to compare notes. She would endorse David and he would return the favor. I'm afraid we had judged her far too hastily. Well, at least I had. She was surprisingly lucid and very smart but maybe a bit too emotional and dramatic. "High-strung" would aptly describe her. We discovered that the members of her HOA adored her and would more than likely vote for her, all 232 registered voters. That might not make a big difference in the mayoral race, but it could put David over the top in Ward 4. We made her an auxiliary member of the A Team without her knowledge or approval. She wouldn't do well at our strategy meetings. She was a teetotaler.

She never really stood a chance against Mayor Winfield. His campaign was run like a machine. Few outside of Tanglewood Estates knew anything about her. But what her candidacy did achieve, and David and Brad both benefited from, was to create a huge distraction for the mayor. He was unable to lend his usual support to his crew. She challenged him to three debates, and he had no choice but to accept. The A Team helped her prepare each time. She did surprisingly well, being a newcomer to the campaign trail. And of course, the *Gazette*, which had endorsed the incumbent, reported that the novice appeared nervous, ill-prepared, and definitely not in the same league as Mayor Winfield. When was Clifford Parks ever known to report the truth?

David campaigned on the need for new blood. His opponent, assuming victory, chose to rest on his laurels. Brad stood firmly on his record of standing up against the mayor and his crew. He had token opposition.

When the clock struck midnight on Election Day, the voters had spoken. Mayor Winfield would return for another two years, defeating our Wendy 71 percent to 29 percent. Brad was re-elected by a large majority. Then there was David. His margin of victory over the incumbent was 106 votes. Wendy may have lost the mayoral war, but with the help of the members of the HOA of Tanglewood Estates, David won the Ward 4 battle.

There was still this numbers problem. The score was now the Crew 4, the Outsiders 4. It seemed likely the mayor was going to have to cast the deciding vote on most issues. Five votes to four. Really, nothing had changed on that front. The mayor would get anything and everything he wanted.

More importantly, the third term of Mayor Warren Winfield would look nothing like the calm, uneventful previous one.

CHAPTER 11

A COUPLE OF THINGS were bugging me. This was Mayor Winfield's third term in office. I had met a lot of very ambitious people and he was at the top of the list. Ambition usually drives people to achieve loftier heights. They crave more power and more control. And yet he seemed to be secure and satisfied in his current role. He was young enough, good-looking enough, and politically savvy enough to go well beyond being the head man in Lenore. The women loved him. A lot of men wanted to be just like him. I'm not sure what there was left for Mayor Winfield to accomplish in Lenore. He was an enigma.

And the second thing was that I knew, as in most towns, there were closed-door meetings, under-the-table deals being offered, and backroom handshakes. Our mayor was more than secretive, he was devious. He could backstab with the best of them. And the old saying fits: "How do you know he's lying? His lips are moving." Even with Brad and David on the council, they were still the Outsiders. They had no idea what he was up to. And I didn't like that one bit.

One evening, after working late preparing for a court date, I had just walked in the door and was starting to relax and enjoy a chilled adult beverage when the phone rang.

"I need a good lawyer. Do you know one?"

It was Judge Jimmy.

"Do you want a good one or an honest one? Can't have both."

After he asked me how the practice was going and I asked him how his family was doing and if he had sentenced any juvenile delinquents to life without parole, I said, "So, Judge Jimmy, what's up?"

"Actually, I do need some legal assistance. My current situation prohibits me from representing myself."

This was not going to be just a friendly call. It sounded like it was important.

"Real estate stuff?"

"In a roundabout way."

Jimmy had been involved with his son-in-law Mike, his oldest daughter's husband, in a continuing residential property venture. They flipped houses. They had established a corporation with Jimmy as the silent partner and the majority investor and Mike handling the construction side. I was their attorney of record. Some of the houses they acquired were in decent shape to start with, while others were downright derelict. And everything in between. Some were abandoned and some were in foreclosure. In addition to being successful, I thought they were doing a great service by saving homes that might otherwise have simply fallen apart, and they were providing relatively low-cost housing to young couples just starting out and to people on a limited income.

"I'm all ears. Just remember my hourly rate, billed in quarter-hour increments."

Ignoring my wise-ass comments, he continued, "We, I mean, the corporation, just received a letter from the town solicitor. She advised us that the property we recently bought on Route 81, just south of the town line, has been declared urban blight."

"Well, that's rather harsh of her."

"There are seven other houses on that short row. Six are occupied and two are empty, ours being one of them. Mike has talked to a couple of the other owners and apparently they all got the same letter."

"I have zero experience in this area, Jimmy. But oddly enough, this was on the bar exam." It had been a long time, but I thought I knew the answer. "Does the word 'condemnation' appear in the letter?"

My serious lawyer side was taking over.

"It does. It says the town is initiating condemnation of the property."

"Right, and do you know what the next step is, Jimmy? I mean, for them. They are going to seize your property under eminent domain laws. It's also called annexation. Of course, you'll receive what is called fair compensation."

Jimmy had a lot of questions.

"Why would they want these homes? Can they do that? This is not my area of expertise. I wish I knew more." I could tell he was very concerned. There was more than a touch of frustration in his voice as well.

"Yep. They sure can. They want the land for something. Maybe road widening. We can try to find out."

"Do we have any legal recourse, Brett?"

"Some. If memory serves, they have to give you a certain amount of time to consult a lawyer. And their offer of fair compensation can be appealed."

"So we've got something at least. You know, Brett, this doesn't hurt Mike and me very much. We don't have a lot tied up in the place we bought. But two or three of those families have been living there for generations. For them, these are not houses, they're homes. Let's hope there's something we can do for them."

I loved this side of Judge Jimmy. This wouldn't be just another real estate transaction for him. For me either, as it turned out.

Because of Jimmy's concern, it became my concern. I wasn't positive about my knowledge of eminent domain law. But I was certain about one thing: our mayor was behind it. But why?

Neither Brad nor David had any knowledge of the move by the town to take these properties, but they said they would try to find out.

I knew I had to do some legal research. I had to learn as much as I could about this eminent domain law.

Saddle up the A Team.

* * *

My research yielded what I had feared. And the news wasn't good. There was little we could do about the property seizures. In eminent domain law, the government could pretty much do as they liked, with few restrictions. Similar to Lenore Bylaw 83dash9dash41, only on a much grander scale.

While I was waiting on information from Brad and David, I met with Jimmy and Mike. We decided on a plan of delaying tactics, mostly to give the affected homeowners some time to make whatever adjustments in their lives they had to make. For Jimmy and Mike it was an opportunity to help some folks who probably couldn't do it themselves. For me, and I certainly wanted to lend a hand as well, it was a chance to throw a monkey wrench into the mayor's agenda.

Nowhere in the letters did it indicate why the homes were being seized, or for what purpose the town intended to use the land. Urban blight was obviously a smoke screen. The homes were not neglected. They were not falling down. They might have been older, but blight they were not. So I filed a show cause motion in Chancery Court in King City. The judge gave the town thirty days to reply.

With Brad's tenure on the council he had made many friends at the town offices who weren't fans of the mayor either. Nothing. No one had any idea what was going on. This was the most closely guarded secret I had ever witnessed.

Mixed in with all my other client work, I spent the next several weeks traveling back and forth to court in King City, filing motion after motion. The judge ruled that the town had to produce the reports of the inspectors who had classified the area as urban blight. I appealed their findings and asked the court to appoint an independent inspector. The judge took my request under advisement. Eventually, as expected, the judge ruled in favor of the town of Lenore.

Our next tactic was to appeal the "fair compensation" offered by the town. I asked the judge to appoint an independent real estate expert to review their offer. We had delayed the final eviction for over 120 days, but I was running out of ideas. I could tell the town solicitor and the judge were losing patience with me. What started out as professional turned into adversarial. Maybe a deadline was fast approaching.

My grandfather had a saying: "You can't fight city hall." And in this case he was right. I had exhausted all options, and finally the judge ruled against any further delays in the property seizures. Eminent domain was a reality for those eight properties out on Route 81.

My trip back to Lenore from the courthouse in King City took me past the homes in question. I had driven this route many times since we started our stall campaign. Then one night it hit me like a brick in the face. From some dark corner of my memory, it came back to me. The notice in the *Gazette* about an option having been taken out on some land on the outskirts of town on Route 81. Could it be the old Barclay place? Did I just hit pay dirt?

The next day I headed for the planning commission office. Land options were supposed to be public knowledge. Or so I thought.

The receptionist advised me that it would require either written permission from the mayor's office, or a court order. Absent either of those documents, she could not give me access to any information regarding any land options. As I was leaving, I looked back to see her making a phone call. The mayor would soon know of my visit and the purpose for same.

But I was a lawyer, and the receptionist at the planning commission was not. After some additional research I discovered there was, in fact, no such requirement to view any land option document. It was public record.

I paid a second visit to the planning commission office. I calmly explained that she was wrong. Nope. She was following instructions from her boss, the commissioner. Conveniently, he was not available. I said I'd wait. When he finally showed up I explained the situation and, once again, I was denied access. I threatened a lawsuit for obstruction and potential termination of his employment. I could tell he was not the type who relished confrontation, and he folded like a cheap lawn chair. I got what I wanted, and I'm sure he got on the phone to the mayor's office.

The land in question was, indeed, the old Barclay place. I had gone to high school with a girl who was a Barclay, so I remembered the name. They had farmed in and around Lenore for decades, starting in the 1920s. Their descendants had no desire to continue in the agricultural business and they had put the land up for sale several years before, unsuccessfully, until now. Things had changed since the announcement in the *Gazette*. There was no longer an option on the property. A final sale had taken place.

The land in question was enormous, hundreds of acres. The party that had taken out the original option was a law firm—Davis, McLean, and Sewell—acting as an agent for an unnamed third party, the eventual buyer. They were located on the West Coast. The best news was that the name of the attorney who signed the original option was printed at the bottom of the document: Clinton Davis. I had an idea.

The next day, I had no trial activities on my daily planner, just a couple of client appointments and a filing with the general sessions court. Frankly, I was glad for a little down time. I have to admit it, business was booming. Sixty-hour weeks were becoming routine. The best part was that I was able to raise my hourly rate. No one complained or even noticed, for that matter. Again, thanks to Peel, my office was the picture of efficiency. And yes, she got a raise.

That day as the clock struck twelve thirty, my tummy reminded me that I needed to eat something and soon. I decided to have lunch at the Chelsea. Funny how your body can often control your decision-making process. For once I wasn't craving a burger and fries from Wally's Drive-In. I needed something healthy. A salad for sure. Maybe some soup. And their chicken salad was the best. It was a nice afternoon, and the Chelsea parking lot was probably full, so I chose to walk. I always enjoyed this ten-minute stroll through downtown Lenore. It was like a quick journey through my past. Most of downtown hadn't changed, structurally. Most of the buildings had been declared historical sites. I often laughed at the thought that those crazy developers who were trying to destroy my town's heritage had been given the middle finger. Nope. Downtown Lenore was off-limits. I made a right turn outside of my office and headed in the direction of the town square. This was my old stomping grounds. I had walked this same sidewalk hundreds of times in my youth. The house I grew up in was still there, on Wilson Street, two blocks on the other side of the square. It was showing signs of age and disrepair, mostly due to a lack of attention paid to it by the current owners. I avoided walking or driving past it. Sadness would overcome me, followed by anger and frustration. Maybe, somewhere down the road, I'd make an offer and be able to buy the place. Among the other things on my wish list, this was right at or near the top.

I turned left on Murray Street and right again on West Main. I recognized all of the buildings and some of the tenants. As I got to the square I passed by the Bank and Trust. I couldn't remember when it wasn't there. I paused for a moment and gazed to my right at the cenotaph, commemorating those souls lost in various wars. There were plaques for World War I, World War II, the Korean War, and Vietnam. This was so much of what I loved about Lenore. We had lost some soldiers in the Middle East. I hoped they would be remembered as well. The courthouse, looming behind, was starting to cast its shadow over the square. A picture postcard.

The Chelsea was just east of the square on Church Street. Its ownership had changed several times over the years, but the layout was exactly the same as I remembered it. On Friday nights we'd all meet at the Chelsea after a high school basketball game. My dad would often treat us to bacon and eggs on a Saturday morning. There had been a jukebox at each booth, a nickel a song. Again, another stop on Memory Lane.

On the way back to the office, with a full stomach and my mind meandering through my past, my relaxed walk was unexpectedly interrupted by Chief Pryor. As I stepped off the curb to cross the street a block from my office, he made a quick U-turn and slammed on his brakes, blocking my path. He couldn't have had a sterner look on his face as he got out of his patrol car.

"We need to talk, Mr. Simmons."

I was seldom able to be serious with this guy.

"My afternoon is full to the brim with lawyer stuff, Chief. Call my office and Peel will set up an appointment for you."

"We'll do this right here."

"On the street across from the Dollar Store? A little unprofessional, don't you think? You're not going to pat me down, are you, Chief?"

The more playful I got, the more serious he became.

"I could arrest you for threatening a town employee."

"And which town employee would that be?" I knew that he knew that I knew.

"The planning commissioner."

"What a coincidence, Chief. I was going to file a complaint against our planning commissioner. I went there on official business, representing a client, and was denied legal access to certain documents."

"What client and what documents, Mr. Simmons?"

I'm sure he already knew what documents I was referencing.

"With your background in law enforcement, I'm surprised you even asked me that. As I was saying, I'm going to file a motion with the court to censure the commissioner and his office for obstruction. I'll have to name the mayor as well."

He looked down at his highly polished shoes. He knew exactly what I was talking about.

"Anything else, Chief?" I got no response. "I guess not. Nice chatting with you."

I headed back to the office, and he probably headed back to the mayor's office to report in.

Being Friday, I waited until 4:55 p.m. Pacific time. On one of those throwaway cell phones, I called Davis, McLean, and Sewell and asked for Clinton Davis by name. "Apologies," the receptionist answered, but Mr. Davis was gone for the day. Then I erupted on the poor guy. I concocted a story that I was with the registrar's office, calling from the town of Lenore, and needed to speak to someone immediately. There had been an error on a document, making the sale of a tract of land null and void, and it would revert to the option, which was going to expire that day. If I couldn't speak to him, then I would need to speak to the client. The young man hesitated. I erupted again. Did he want the expiration of the option to be put on his shoulders? I could hear the click of fingers on a keyboard. In a few seconds, he gave me a phone number. West Coast as well. I thanked him for his cooperation.

I was questioning the whys of Mayor Winfield's activities. At some point I knew I had to question my own motives. How important was this for me, personally, to risk everything I had achieved, and I mean my career (read: license to practice law)? Was it worth it? As an officer of the court I was sworn to uphold the law. Impersonation of a public official, either in person or by phone, was a misdemeanor punishable by a fine not to exceed $10,000 and potential jail time. I already knew the answer. Where I lived, where I worked was Lenore. My sense of right and wrong would never let me sit back and just allow whatever this was to go on. I couldn't bury my head in the sand or turn a blind eye and pretend everything was in the normal range. Nope, not this guy. The needle was way over on the red and my conscience wouldn't stand for it. So I decided to put my phone call performance on my tab, along with uttering threats to an employee of the town of Lenore. There was more to come. When you wrestle an alligator, you have to get down in the muck and the mud. And it appeared that I was indeed about to wrestle an alligator. The personal cost for me could be enormous. But yes, from the beginning, I knew it was worth it.

I called the second West Coast number. I got the standard message.

"Thank you for calling Pegasus Financial Group. Our offices are currently closed. Please leave a message at the sound of the tone and your call will be returned."

I had a name: Pegasus Financial Group.

Then I decided to jerk their chain. So I left a message, in my best imitation Southern drawl.

"This here's Sam Dawson, over in Lenore. Warren Winfield, the mayor, now he's a good friend, he told me that you fellas have purchased the old Barclay place out on Route 81. I'm lookin' for some more land to graze my cows and I was hopin' we could make some kind of lease arrangement. I'll just call back on Monday. Thanks much."

Someone was bound to listen to that message on Monday morning. No one was supposed to be able to connect Pegasus with this land deal. Apparently, some farmer named Sam Dawson did. I was hoping for a reaction. Not sure what, exactly. And after our mayor was advised of the message I had left and add to that the fact that he had no friend by the name of Sam Dawson, it wouldn't take a rocket scientist to figure out it was one Brett Simmons who had made that call.

It didn't take long for the cow patties to hit the fan.

CHAPTER 12

I HAD TO MEET with the A Team, and yes, it was Friday evening. No one even hinted at a complaint. I liked that. I went over the details of my discoveries. When asked how I came to acquire such information, I pleaded the fifth. All I said was that I made a couple of strategic, although borderline-illegal calls to the West Coast, but I did not want to make them coconspirators, or codefendants, or accessories after the fact. If I was going down with the ship, I would do so alone. After all, they were duly elected officials and I was just the official boil on the butt of the mayor. Maybe he should see someone about that. And he did.

I volunteered to find out all I could about the law firm and Pegasus. Anything and everything. Brad and David were to continue digging up whatever they could at the municipal offices, which so far hadn't produced any tangible information. We all agreed on one thing, which was really a question that hovered over us: Why all the secrecy? Land deals occur all the time. It was standard practice for developers to take options out on properties, then purchase the land. Eminent domain law was commonplace. Normally there was no need for all the hush-hush. What could they possibly be hiding? We threw out all kinds of theories, few of which made any sense.

Funny thing, right before we broke up for the night Brad asked me if whatever it was I had done had put me in any danger and I'd laughed it off.

"No, of course not," I'd replied.

I may have sounded confident on the outside. Inside I wasn't so sure.

I had hoped that my Saturday would be restful and uneventful and that I would wake up with nothing to do, and I wouldn't get to that until about noon. Nope. My phone rang at eight thirty. I was in my T-shirt and boxers, on my couch, comfortably enjoying a cup of freshly brewed Italian coffee as I watched a *Miami Vice* rerun. My caller ID said it was David Spencer. For a second I thought about ignoring it. But you know me, I had to answer it.

"You up for a brisk ride this morning, Counselor?"

I wanted him to know, without actually saying it, that I wasn't in the mood to be disturbed.

"I am not. I am up for doing exactly what I'm doing now."

"And that would be?"

"Nothing."

Apparently, David didn't care how I felt about his call. He just kept on talking.

"Do you know what my brother-in-law does for a living, sport?"

"Nope, and I don't give a flip."

I mean, how much more obvious could I get? I wanted to be left alone. But David was being David.

"Be ready in thirty minutes." And he hung up.

I admit that I was in a lousy mood. I had experienced one of those nights where no part of my dreams made sense. Mallory McCutcheon made her usual appearance. What? Where was that coming from? To this day I don't understand it. She was sixteen the last time I saw her. This made no sense. Then I was standing in front of the other eight justices of the Supreme Court, arguing why I shouldn't be recalled following a complaint from Warren Winfield. Not an ounce of reality here. I guess it must have been the tacos I ate for dinner. I think I woke up right about then, confused and angry, with a serious case of heartburn. No more late-night tacos for me. It was 5:00 a.m. and I was still exhausted. Sleep had turned its back on me, so I got up.

I was in no disposition to entertain David Spencer and whatever he had planned for me.

But, like one of Pavlov's dogs, and after a handful of Tums, I did shower and shave. I was ready in about twenty-five minutes.

As soon as I got into his car I turned to him and, in a not-so-friendly tone, said, "I hope this special event you're taking me to is catered." My stomach had settled down and I was jonesing for some pancakes or eggs Benedict.

David was happier to see me than I was to see him. "You're chipper this morning. Slept well, I see."

I just stared straight ahead. I didn't want to be there and I didn't want to do this. So I responded with my usual flair: "And the horse you rode in on!"

David continued, undeterred, "We—that is, you and I and my brother-in-law—are going for a ride."

"Where?"

"I tried to tell you what he did for a living and you said you didn't care."

At least David got that message.

"I don't. Sometimes, David, when honesty is the best policy, it is not well received."

"So you know, you jackwagon, Drew is a helicopter pilot. Specifically, he flies a Medivac chopper for King City Memorial Hospital."

"Good for him." David didn't see me roll my eyes.

"We're headed to the K.C. airport, where he is standing by with a borrowed chopper. Any ideas where we might be going, Counselor?"

Sleep deprivation is a condition that most people don't handle easily. Count me as one of those. Then add in my crazy dreams with a case of taco heartburn and you've got yourself a grumpy, uncooperative lawyer who is not capable of putting two and two together. But finally I was able to figure it out and that jump-started my brain.

"We're going to take a ride over the Barclay place."

David just laughed.

"You can move to the head of the class and be the teacher's pet again."

He got an icy stare in return.

"Sort of, Brett. We're going to fly near the farm, within viewing distance, to see what's going on, if anything."

"Will they get suspicious?"

"I doubt it. There's air traffic buzzing around all the time. It's Saturday and lots of pleasure pilots with their baby Cessnas filling up our local air space. As long as we don't fly directly over the farm, I think we'll be OK."

My flying experience is limited. Let's just say I find myself at an airport, coming or going, only when necessary. Sarah and I honeymooned in Jamaica, so of course we flew. I made an annual pilgrimage—by air—to visit my parents, and I had flown to a couple of law school reunions. So don't put me down as one who hates flying or is scared to fly. I'm not uncomfortable in an airplane, and I'm not one of those white-knucklers on takeoff and landing. But the truth is, I had never been inside of nor lifted off the ground in a helicopter. This was definitely a new experience for me. I was used to rumbling down a runway at a speed of over a hundred knots, then slowly lifting off the ground. Drew, David's brother-in-law, must have sensed my less than excited attitude as I strapped myself into the seat next to him. Or what was probably closer to the truth, David put him up to it. One minute we're sitting on the ground going over safety systems and procedures, the next we went straight up in the air at breathtaking speed, leaving my stomach and its contents on the ground below. I was the only one on board that helicopter who wasn't laughing.

After Drew's half-hearted attempt to apologize to me between fits of laughter, we leveled off at about a thousand feet and headed south. We stayed west of Route 81 and made a wide circle over Lenore. I was able to recover my bearings, both physically and emotionally, and I could now recognize landmarks.

I must have been in the sixth or seventh grade when I saw my first aerial photographs of Lenore. From what I remember, there was the town and not much else, only farmland. Now the urban sprawl was everywhere. There was still some farmland remaining on the fringes, but, for the most part, I saw roads and rooftops. I admit it was a depressing sight. It was easy to recognize the town square and the courthouse. I even spotted my office building. Drew made a slow left-hand turn, then headed north, continuing to stay to the west of Route 81. He dropped his airspeed as we approached the target to our right. He pointed out Townline Road, which ran west to east, abutting the north edge of the Barclay property. From what I could tell, things were moving quickly below us. There appeared to be a fence surrounding the entire property, probably a recent addition. Hard to tell what kind or how high it was. There was one main structure, a barn, with some other smaller buildings. The barn appeared to be older, perhaps left over from the Barclay family. On the west side of the property a gravel lane led from Barclay Side Road to the barn. The side road ran north and south. But the most interesting thing, from our vantage point, was the outline of what Drew thought looked like a landing strip of some kind, running diagonally across the property, with a taxiway leading to the back side of the barn. That's what it looked like to David and me as well. There was plenty of earth-moving equipment all over the property, but no agricultural implements that we could see and no aircraft. Being a Saturday, it was reasonable that there was no human activity that we could detect. Pegasus was not going to sit on this property. It was going to be used for something, and that something probably involved airplanes.

The drive over to the airport took longer than our jaunt in the chopper. As soon as we landed, I called Brad. I filled him in with what we had seen and our initial conclusions.

"They aren't going to farm that land, are they, Brett?"

"Not in the normal way, Brad, I don't think. That runway, or what's left of it, is probably at the center of all this."

Our call ended, again with more questions than answers.

After a not-so-restful Sunday, Monday was busy. I was having a late lunch after I had spent the morning in court in King City. I was wolfing down a burger from Wally's Drive-In when Peel put a call through. It was Brad.

"Buckle up, Counselor, we're going wheels up."

I had no idea what he was talking about. "English please, Brad."

"Our beloved mayor has just left for the K.C. airport, heading due west. His office claims he's on a fact-finding junket, meeting with unknown business-types who may want to invest in our fair town. And he's traveling on the town's dime."

"And that's BS, Brad."

There's no way you set up a quick face-to-face with a potential investor. BS for sure. And Brad agreed.

"Yep. I guess whatever that quasi-illegal thing you did on Friday woke somebody up, and I believe the mayor is paying a hastily arranged visit."

That made me smile.

"I'm getting this sense, Brad, that maybe there's some cracks showing up in their foundation."

Brad had some more news.

"And know what else?"

I was glad I was sitting down. "Hit me."

"The mayor is not traveling alone."

I guess I shouldn't have been surprised. But I was.

"Really!"

Brad continued, "It seems a Crew member is accompanying Mr. Winfield on this important trip."

Brad was acting like a news anchor simply giving the headlines. I needed the rest of the story.

"And who might that be?"

Brad paused for a second to add a little more drama to the moment and then spit it out. "The one and only Mrs. Dana Parks, formerly Crew member number five, now number four."

I realized there was another side to this story.

"And the good and loyal Mrs. Winfield has been left behind to keep the home fires burning."

"Something like that. Oh, and Brett, just so you know, the council meeting for tomorrow night has been canceled."

How silly of me to think otherwise. No mayor, no meeting.

The mayor's impromptu West Coast trip got my imagination running at full speed. I could picture him and his accomplice—I mean, traveling partner—Mrs. Parks, sitting in some office trying to explain why some clerk in Lenore had a problem with the sale documents for the Barclay farm and how a friend of his, a farmer named Sam Dawson, found out about Pegasus. I'm sure at some point the conversation became heated. And I'm just as sure my name came up eventually.

And speaking of my imagination, sometimes, out of the blue, I'll get a crazy idea that I just have to explore. Most of the time it's an exercise in futility, but not always. I asked Peel if we had any back issues of the *Gazette*, say, from the past eight weeks or so. She returned with about twelve weeks' worth. We went through each one and circled any picture in which the mayor appeared. I knew that the *Gazette* loved to show our leader in action, and what politician would pass up the chance for a photo op.

In twenty-four issues of the *Gazette* our mayor's picture appeared in every one of them, a total of sixty-one times. He was photographed alone only nine times. Out of the remaining fifty-two shots, there was a common denominator in forty-three of them. Accompanying him was none other than Crew Member #4, Mrs. Dana Parks, and in most of them she was looking up at him adoringly. I wondered if Mr. Parks saw what I saw. Mrs. Winfield was conspicuous in her absence. She appeared in none of the photos. Zero.

Later that night, I took full advantage of my LexisNexis subscription, a great online research tool and a lawyer's best friend. It's like having a research assistant on call 24-7. I was able to give the team a report on the esteemed law firm of Davis, McLean, and Sewell and, of course, Pegasus Financial Group. The firm, on the surface, appeared to be a big-time outfit with offices all over the place and dozens of partners and associates. Lots of glitz and gloss. The reality was they had one office with three partners and few support people. Not a major player. They were known to represent foreign entities, and on their website they advertised themselves as advocates for the global marketplace. One of their partners, the headliner Mr. Clint Davis, had been suspended from practicing law reportedly for using his clients' escrow accounts as his own, to the tune of $1.5 million. Within the last year, he had made full restitution and he had recently been reinstated. I wondered about three things: How did a pissant, little firm like this get someone to give them $1.5 million in the first place? Why hadn't Mr. Davis gone to jail for embezzlement? And where did he get that kind of money to repay the debt? All legitimate questions that needed to be asked. I figured it was somebody who knew somebody who had access to a lot of money to throw around—legal or otherwise. I would have bet on the otherwise. What I wouldn't have given to know the who and the why. This Clint Davis is the reason folks quote William Shakespeare. Not that I have ever read any of Bill's works, but I heard that he once said, "The first thing we're going to do is kill all the lawyers." Not sure if that's an exact quote, but close enough. When the executions start, I hope this guy is first in line.

And next was Pegasus Financial Group. Oddly enough, their address was in the same building as the law firm, one floor below. Things that make you go "hmmm." They were listed as a private equity company. They bought and sold other companies, several of which I was able to find. Nothing of note. They also brokered real estate deals. Here we go.

There were several insignificant property transactions, none any more recent than three years before. It appeared that the company was dormant, which I knew it wasn't. Obviously, this new transaction involving the Barclay place hadn't made it to their record, if it ever would. But the most interesting detail was that Pegasus was registered as being foreign owned, with majority ownership being held by an unnamed company in Brazil. I wouldn't have been surprised if the $1.5 million borrowed by Mr. Clint Davis had originated in Rio de Janeiro or São Paulo.

The plot, as they say, thickens.

CHAPTER 13

WHEN I STARTED THIS campaign of civil harassment of the mayor and his crew, I did so more tongue in cheek than with the intention of causing havoc at town hall. I enjoyed sparring with Chief Pryor and Sergeant Stuckey, at least at first. They served at the pleasure of the mayor. He was their boss and they did what they were told. It didn't take long to realize that, in the same way, the editor/owner of the *Gazette* was under the influence of his wife, Crew Member #4. It was obvious she called the shots in public, and there was no reason to believe their relationship was any different behind closed doors, both at home and at the newspaper. I had no idea that my involvement and that of my partners in crime, David and Brad, would lead to the intrigue and mystery in which we would soon find ourselves.

That question of why was still hovering over us like a dark cloud before a storm. We may not have been very sophisticated, but at the very least we were intelligent. There was something we were missing. Maybe it was right in front of us. Maybe we needed to enlist more help, people who could look into the dark corners that were inaccessible to us.

A few days after the mayor and his business associate had returned from their successful trip to the West Coast, we received some unsolicited assistance. Brad was approached by Outsider Bow Tie Denny. He was furious that the mayor had used municipal funds for his excursion and even more livid that #4 had gone with him. He was able to gain access to the mayor's expense report. Surprise! They paid over $300 per night for their hotel that happened to be right down the street from the building that housed our new friends, Pegasus and the law firm. Not sure if it was one suite or two. Hmmm, good for them.

Brad recommended that we add Bow Tie Denny to our group. I was not enthusiastic about the idea, but after Brad's assurances that he would be a huge asset, I agreed, as did David. Then there were four.

I guess I'm not much of a judge of character. First it was Wendy Tolliver. Now, I was so wrong about Bow Tie Denny. He brought more to the table than I ever imagined he would. His passion was infectious, and his knowledge was vast. If Lenore had a historian, it was Bow Tie. And he really knew the system, how things worked at town hall. He was not the loose cannon I had imagined. I liked him.

We brought him up to speed with what we knew and, more importantly, what we didn't know, which was the why. It was Bow Tie who asked the question of all questions: "Why that particular tract of land? Why on Route 81?" We all agreed that the landing strip probably had a lot to do with it, but there were so many attractive and available parcels of land in Lenore and the surrounding area. He volunteered to dig a little deeper on our behalf.

The next morning, Brad called to tell me there was going to be a significant announcement at a press conference in the council chambers at 10:00 a.m. One of my suspicions would be confirmed. The mayor proudly declared that some land had been purchased by the town to allow the construction of a new road connecting Route 81 with Barclay Side Road. According to the mayor, it was long overdue and had the potential of opening up new opportunities for economic growth. He declined to take questions from anyone following the announcement, citing a conference call for which he was running late. You didn't have to be a genius to figure out that the new connector road would lead directly to the tract of land in question. Missing from the announcement, conspicuous in their absence, at least to me, were what had become my two least favorite legal words, eminent domain.

And then Bow Tie Denny substantiated another one of our suspicions. He had done a little historical digging. As David and I had seen from the air, running diagonally across the entire property was a landing strip, long abandoned, overgrown, and at this point probably unusable, but more than functional in the not-too-distant future. It had been built after World War II by one of the Barclay boys returning home. He had been a fighter pilot and apparently fell in love with flying. He was able to purchase a small aircraft and later built the airfield. It had fallen into disrepair after his death in the 1990s. Bow Tie was certain the airstrip was the deciding factor in Pegasus's choice of land.

And there was something else, something that appeared to be insignificant at the time: an invitation that both David and Brad received.

Merle Atkinson suddenly announced his retirement as the mayor's driver/ bodyguard. After thirty-five years of service to the town of Lenore and its mayors, and with weakening eyesight, Merle decided to hand in his keys to the mayor's new limo. He wanted to spend more time with his grandkids. Good for him. The mayor hosted a buffet luncheon on his behalf in the banquet room at the Chelsea. An invitation never made it to the Law Offices of Brett Simmons. Peel intimated that it must have been lost in the mail. Uh-huh.

What did become significant was Merle's replacement. Whereas Merle was more driver than bodyguard, the newbie was definitely the opposite judging from the bulge underneath his left arm, concealed by his black suit coat. I suspect he never left home without them, his best friends, Mr. Smith and Mr. Wesson. Tall, jet-black hair, and most definitely he never met a weight room he didn't like. And with the aviator sunglasses he made quite the imposing figure. He became the mayor's shadow. Where Warren Winfield went, you could count on Rambo, as we initially called him, to be right there. From what danger he was protecting the mayor was pure conjecture. Although I never talked to him, those who did reported that he spoke with a strange and heavy accent.

What was going on? Two questions may have been answered. Eight houses would be torn down to make room for a new cloverleaf on Route 81. The airstrip was probably why they chose the Barclay place. No other property within the town limits of Lenore, at least that we knew of, had an airstrip. What would they be doing there that would require airplanes to take off and land, and again, why all the secrecy?

I did have an additional asset that had slipped my mind. During the bribery and conspiracy investigation of Mayor Marty, I had made the acquaintance of an investigator with the attorney general's office. He had left me his business card and told me to call him if I needed his help. He was about to hear from me for the second time.

CHAPTER 14

CLAY BONNER WAS A no-nonsense cop. He played hardball with Mayor Marty and the others in the building inspection scam. He returned my call within the hour. I gave him the Readers' Digest version of Mayor Winfield, Pegasus, the law firm, and, most importantly, the airstrip. He took notes. I told him I didn't think they had done anything illegal yet. He agreed, but the whole secrecy thing bothered him as much as it did me. The question of why. He said that when he had the time, he'd do some poking around for us. I wasn't sure he could help us, but I was certain at that point that we were spinning our wheels and anything he could do for us would be more than we already had.

I still had to make a living at my chosen profession. Bills to pay, you know, rent, groceries, and Peel expected a paycheck every two weeks. Trips to King City were normal in my practice. We had municipal court, traffic court, and juvenile court in Lenore, and that was about it. Anything beyond that required a visit to K.C., the county seat. After a long day in family court I had stayed to enjoy the evening with a lawyer friend, Carrie Kincade. She was definitely a friend with benefits. She was a former assistant district attorney. Our early encounters were not pleasant. She won the first case on behalf of the prosecution, then I won the next two on behalf of my clients. We were adversaries, professionally speaking. Then she left public service for private practice, and let's just say, our relationship blossomed.

On this particular night, at about nine thirty, with a smile that went from one ear to the other, I headed back to Lenore on Route 81. There was little traffic that time of night, so I put the Honda on cruise control and tried to enjoy the quiet ride. I had just passed the conservation area when I saw headlights in my rearview mirror, closing the gap between us fast. I mean, fast. The car came right up behind me, bumper to bumper, NASCAR-style. I felt a bump, then another one. My heart was pounding in my chest. This idiot clearly intended to run me off the road. He backed off for a few seconds. Then he bumped me again, and again, and this time I almost lost control. Terror quickly changed to anger. When he bumped me again, I touched my brakes enough so he could see my brake lights. He backed off. A few seconds later he was back. I started yelling at him. Not sure why. He couldn't hear me. I touched my brakes again, and this time I started to slow down. He didn't bump me, he banged into me. I sped up again. So did he. We had just passed the Welcome to Lenore sign when he pulled into the oncoming lane right beside me. The windows were tinted; I couldn't see in his car. He stayed there for a few miles, then he sped up, swerving back into the right lane in an attempt to cut me off. Then it hit me that he might have a weapon aimed right at me. I slammed on the brakes and came to a stop on the shoulder of the road. He was gone. I was sweating profusely and not only were my hands shaking, my entire body was trembling. It took me a few minutes to recover before I could head back home. My hands were still quivering when I drank my first beer. As you can imagine, Mr. Sandman did not visit Brett Simmons that night.

Things had happened so fast, I failed to get the license plate number. All I know is that it was a late-model Chevrolet, maybe beige in color, with some newly acquired damage to the front bumper. For the next few weeks, I looked all over town, but with no success. The Chevy and the driver were probably long gone. But what was left behind was the nagging thought about the calls I had made to the law firm and Pegasus. It would be a safe assumption that this was not a random act. Hardly. Whoever had been driving the Chevy certainly was familiar with my car and my driving habits. They had known where I was and which route I would take on my way home. It could have been far worse for me. I struggled to put that thought out of my mind. One thing I can say with certainty, they knew I had made those calls to the West Coast and I had their attention.

I shared my experience with David, Brad, and Bow Tie. Things were heating up and not in a good way. Had we poked the bear? Did we wake the sleeping giant? It appeared so. I put in a call to Clay Bonner. He listened intently as I described the incident. Then came the questions.

"Road rage, Brett?"

"I hardly think so. If he wanted to pass me, he could have. There was no other traffic on the road."

"You were targeted?"

That's the only answer I had. "We have to assume that to be the case."

"Could he have killed you if he'd wanted to?"

As much as I didn't want to, I had to admit it. "Absolutely."

"I think it was a shot across your bow."

"Warning?"

"Yep. Listen, Brett, I have to testify in court over the next few days. Then, after that, you've got my undivided attention."

Three days later he called back. He said that the judge had issued a gag order and was allowing the defense attorneys latitude with some newly discovered evidence.

"Don't know how long this is going to take, Brett. I'm sending someone down there. Agent's name is Mel. One of my best."

"Thanks, Clay. I appreciate your help."

He didn't say when I should expect Mel's arrival.

* * *

Two days later, as was the norm, I was busy being a lawyer. Not all legal work is done in court. Most of my billing hours were accumulated sitting behind my pre-owned desk. Under normal circumstances, with no clients occupying the guest chairs in my office, I would leave the door open. As I often did when I was on the phone, I turned my chair so I could look out the window behind me, leaving my back toward the door. I had just hung up the phone and turned back around, and frankly I was startled.

Standing in my doorway was a tall, well-dressed lady with medium-long auburn hair. She was wearing black slacks and a white blouse with a dark gray jacket. No necklace. Small gold ear studs. Her makeup was barely noticeable. Did I say she was tall? She had legs for days!

After my initial surprise at seeing her standing there, I judged her to be not unattractive. Peel was standing behind her, just to the right enough for me see her mouthing the word "sorry." I nodded my approval and she went back to her desk.

"I thought I'd drop by, Mr. Simmons. Busy?"

"Not now. And you are?"

"I'm Melanie Stockton."

"Congratulations, Ms. Stockton. How can I help you?"

"Did Clay Bonner not advise you that I was coming?"

You don't hear the term *male chauvinist* much anymore. I mean, I've been called that on several occasions, but not in a very long time. It seemed to fit this current situation. Clay had said he was sending an agent named Mel. So I assumed, chauvinistically, that it was a guy whose full name was Melvin. My bad.

"He did, but I'm a little embarrassed—"

She cut me off in mid sentence. "And you were expecting some guy named Mel. Clay does that all the time. It's his sick sense of humor."

I thought, Wait until you get a load of mine, lady.

"By now you've guessed that Mel is short for Melanie."

"And here you are. Clay said you're one of his best agents."

I got up, went around my desk, and walked toward her with my hand extended.

She was tall indeed. She stood maybe three inches below my six, one.

After we shook hands, I motioned for her to take a seat.

"So, Agent Stockton, would you agree with Clay that you are one of his best?" Probably a dumb, probing question on my part, but there it was, out of my mouth.

I guess the question could have been construed as a request for her résumé or at least some proof that Clay wasn't just blowing smoke in my face, considering his reputation for having, according to Melanie Stockton, a sick sense of humor. But if she was embarrassed by my question, she didn't show it.

"Let's just say that I'm good at my job, very good. I started out as a uniformed cop on the street in Indianapolis, chasing thugs from one end of the city to the other. I was promoted to detective after four years. After solving several high-profile cases in the Criminal Investigation Division, I came to the attention of Clay Bonner and I chose to join his staff at the AG's office. My specialty is investigating municipal corruption, among other things. There are several former politicians, currently behind bars, who don't think very highly of me. I have been part of Clay's team for eight years. And on a personal note, I grew up with four older brothers, so I can cuss like a sailor and I enjoy warm beer and cold pizza for breakfast. I drink my bourbon with one cube of ice. If I'm buying, it's Woodford Reserve. If someone else is picking up the tab, their choice. I don't do cigarettes, but I'll smoke a cigar if the opportunity presents itself. Should I choose to pursue it, I would qualify as a sniper. In short, Mr. Simmons, I am my own person and I can take care of myself. But make no mistake, I'm still a lady. I'll leave it at that."

She was done, and I made a mental note not to piss this lady off.

"I'm glad that you're here." I wasn't making that up. I was really happy to see her.

"And I'm glad to be back at work."

I assumed she had taken a little R & R. I was wrong. Dead wrong.

"Vacation?"

"Not exactly." She paused. I sensed she was struggling to continue. "Administrative leave."

And as expected, my mouth was in gear well ahead of my brain.

"So what naughty thing did you do to get yourself put in time-out?"

At first she looked down at the floor. Then she got up and walked over to the window, where she stared outside for a few seconds, her eyes fixed on nothing in particular. After a few moments she turned and looked at me. "I shot a suspect."

I wanted to find a hole and jump in it. Way to go, Brett. My attempt at humor completely missed its mark. I've known this lady for barely a few minutes and I've already made an ass of myself.

"I'm so sorry. That was totally inappropriate of me."

"It's OK. You had no way of knowing."

It wasn't OK. I was afraid that I had upset her.

Looking right into my eyes, very matter-of-factly she continued, "They put me on leave for ninety days. It's automatic when an officer fires his or her weapon. I went through the required psychological testing and I've been cleared to return to duty. They investigated the incident and it was declared a justified shooting."

I had a notion that there was more to her story, but without a doubt, this lady was the real deal. Nothing pretentious about her. And the best part was that she was standing in my office, ready to take up our cause.

"With the introductions complete, I'm ready to get started. You?" There was resolve in the tone of her voice.

I nodded in agreement.

"Did Clay bring you up to speed on this weird situation here in Lenore?"

"He did. I'll probably require some additional background as we proceed."

I had been leading the charge in this whole affair, and I was certainly glad to hand over the reins to someone who knew what they were doing. But I wanted her to understand that I wasn't there to be a spectator. Little did I know.

"Let me know what you need from me."

"I will. I took the initiative and contacted some friends at the federal level. I'm owed some favors, so I decided to collect."

"Thanks."

"What's up with Lenore and its mayors?" That was certainly a legitimate question that I couldn't answer.

"You got me." First Mayor Marty and now this clown, Warren Winfield. I had no idea.

"I'm not sure it's a good idea for folks to know I'm here, at least not yet."

I knew what "folks" she was talking about.

"How long are you staying?"

"As long as it takes. I'd like to stay in town if possible, to stay close by."

A good thought, but logistically a problem.

"We have a couple of decent hotels, but you would have to check in and someone might ask questions. This is a small town."

"Good point. How about your place? Got a spare room?"

I thought at first she was kidding, so I went along.

"Would your husband approve?"

She held up her left hand, displaying no ring.

"Boyfriend?"

"If I had one, it would be none of his business. What about Mrs. Simmons?"

"What does my mother have to do with this?"

"I was inquiring about your wife."

"I haven't had any contact with my ex-wife in quite some time."

"So my bunking down at your place would create no awkward situations?"

She wasn't kidding. So I took one more salvo to see how serious she was.

"Other than I sleep in the nude and I've been known to sleepwalk. If you're OK with that, *mi casa, su casa*. Oh, and room service sucks."

The sleeping in the nude thing was not exactly accurate. Boxers and a T-shirt for me. Same with the sleepwalking. I discovered that I couldn't handle the sight of my own naked body first thing in the morning, or at least until I had my first cup of coffee. I was just trying to get a reaction.

None was forthcoming. She did have four older brothers.

She smiled. "I'll take it. What will the neighbors think?"

Not that I cared what my neighbors thought, but I did respond: "That my choice in female companionship has improved dramatically."

"I'll take that as a compliment, Mr. Simmons."

"Please call me Brett. Do you prefer Melanie or Mel, or strictly formal, Ms. Stockton?"

"Normally, Agent Stockton, but you remind me a little of our friend, Clay. So Mel it is."

"And I'll take that as a compliment, Mel."

"Do you know what nickname Clay has chosen for you?"

"I can hardly wait to find out."

She had this odd grin on her face that I found very sexy.

"The Ninja Warrior! I'd love to hear how that came about."

"My lips are sealed. Well, they unseal after a few beers, so let that be a warning to you."

"Duly warned." And there was that grin again.

And then quickly back to the business at hand.

"I need to make a few calls, Brett."

"You can use the conference room here."

"Thanks."

So old Clay set me up, but I did feel much more at ease. I don't scare easily, but the bumper-car episode made me sit up and take notice. Hopefully, having a house guest who could probably shoot the left nut off a mosquito at a thousand meters would be a welcome distraction.

It would take a call from an unexpected source to start the snowball rolling downhill. And what started out as a tiny ball of frozen precipitation in my hand would eventually become a full-scale avalanche.

CHAPTER 15

EIGHTY-FOUR DEGREES WITH A light breeze blowing, we had just come in from a refreshing swim in the Mediterranean. Carrie Kincade had asked me to towel off her back when I heard the most annoying beeping sound. It wouldn't stop. I woke up. Damn it, my cell phone. It read 12:51 a.m. I didn't recognize the number.

Not amused at being called at that hour, I barked into the phone, "Simmons."

"Mr. Simmons, I need to meet with you. Tomorrow, behind the old Merrifield building. Ten a.m."

It was a male voice. He sounded out of breath, or maybe he was terrified, or both.

"Who is this?"

"I have some information regarding the property on Route 81. Key word is 'fact.'" Then he hung up.

I was still far from being awake, but I sat on the edge of the bed. I hadn't recognized the voice at all.

Merrifield Industries had moved their operation to Mexico several years before. Their former building had been vacant ever since. And what did he mean by 'key word'? Maybe this was a setup. But it would be in broad daylight and I'd have Sniper Mel as backup.

I'm not sure how long it took me to fall back asleep, but eventually I did. Same dream, at least initially. Wearing only a towel, Carrie Kincade was holding up a dress in each hand, wanting to know which one I preferred. I preferred that she remove the towel. Then a siren was screaming. It wouldn't stop. All of a sudden, Carrie and I were in a car and we were being chased by a beige Chevrolet. Rambo—the one with the heavy accent—was driving. He had a wild look on his face. Then I woke up again, this time in a cold sweat. The sound of the siren was real and it began to fade into the distance. Dawn was forcing its way into my room, sneaking past the drawn curtains. I checked my phone. It was 5:45. I got up and headed for the shower. A cold shower, thank you, Carrie Kincade.

* * *

I was on my second cup of coffee, maybe the third. Mel was on her first. Apparently, she'd slept far better than I had. After I told her about the middle-of-the-night call, she motioned with her hand that she wanted details.

"You didn't recognize his voice."

"Nope." I had been racking my brain, but I couldn't put a name or a face to the voice.

"You've still got the number on your phone."

"Yes." I showed it to her.

"I'll run it to see who it belongs to."

Just as we were getting ready to leave for the office, my phone rang again. It was David.

"I just got to the municipal offices. Did you hear the news?"

I wasn't sure. News does travel fast in a town like Lenore. Did he want me to confirm that I'd had a pajama party with an unknown female?

"What news?"

"They found Clifford Parks, the editor of the *Gazette*. Dead. Chief Pryor said it appears to be a hit-and-run."

I immediately thought about the late-model Chevrolet. That could have been me. I tried to sound calm, but inside, I was far from it. "Where?" I asked.

"On the side street next to the old Merrifield building."

What was Clifford Parks doing at the Merrifield building in the middle of the night?

"Alright, David, we need to meet. Now. See if you can round up Brad and Bow Tie. My office. I want you to meet someone."

Just as I hung up with David, Mel got a call. She listened for a few seconds, then hung up.

"Got the mystery caller's name. The number belongs to a Mr. Clifford Parks."

Now the pieces started to fit together. But our meeting was for ten o'clock. I was confused.

One thing I knew for sure, so I told Mel. "Our ten a.m. meeting has been canceled. That siren we talked about that we heard early this morning—they found Mr. Parks dead. Apparently, a hit-and-run."

Mel responded with that cop's tone in her voice: "Apparently, a hit-and-run, Brett, but was it an accident or a homicide?"

* * *

At the office, I introduced the A Team to Agent Melanie Stockton. I told them about the call from the now deceased Clifford Parks. You could've heard a pin drop. Whatever it was that the editor/owner had wanted to share would be taken to the grave with him. We were back to square one, basically.

David spoke up: "So he was murdered."

Mel answered, "I would say odds are against it being an accident. The autopsy should clear that up, one way or the other."

You could almost taste the tension in the room. For a moment, we all just stared at each other.

"Are we in any danger? Us, our families?" Brad asked.

With a firm, but reassuring tone, Mel took over. "Let's not take any chances. I'm going to get some additional agents down here pronto. I'll make sure you get around-the-clock protection."

Both David and Brad had to break this news to their wives. That was not going to go over well.

Here we go again. On the surface there had been nothing illegal going on, at least not until my car chase, and now this.

By midafternoon, Lenore had some additional visitors. Mel's posse had arrived.

CHAPTER 16

PRIOR TO THE ARRIVAL of Mel's good guys, she decided to shake things up by paying a courtesy visit to Chief Pryor to advise him that an investigation was in progress, ordered by the attorney general's office, which wasn't exactly true. As I was beginning to find out, Agent Stockton had a knack for embellishing the truth, but in a good way. I waited in the lobby. She told the chief that, at least for the time being, she couldn't give him details other than to say that additional resources were being sent in and there was no need to involve the Lenore Police Department. However, should it become necessary, less than full cooperation from the department would be met with severe consequences. The chief nodded his acknowledgment.

Mel was sure that as soon as she left the chief's office, the mayor's phone would be blowing up, which was the sole purpose of her visit in the first place. We walked across the town square and stood in the shadows with the front of the municipal offices in full view. In less than five minutes the mayor emerged—without his sidekick, Rambo—and walked hurriedly across the square and into the Lenore Bank and Trust. He came back out about five minutes later and walked directly to the municipal office.

We continued to watch to see if anything else developed. Sure enough, a car pulled up in front of the bank. And guess who got out? The grieving widow, Crew Member #4. Apparently a pretty red-print dress was appropriate attire for a mourner. She went into the bank and within a few minutes she came back out, got in the car, and drove away.

I turned to Mel. "What I wouldn't give to know what they were doing in the bank."

"My guess is they were making tactical cash withdrawals. I'm going to say about nine thousand dollars each."

"Why?"

"Just a hunch, but you can't leave the country with more than ten thousand dollars in unreported cash."

"You think they're jumping ship?"

"I've seen it before."

Maybe she had, but I hadn't. And I'm the lawyer here. A little awkward for me. Why didn't I know that, about the money?

"Anything we can do, Mel?"

"Not legally. They haven't broken any laws. I can go to my bank and take out nine thousand dollars. Nothing wrong with that."

"You've got nine thousand dollars?"

In addition to that sexy grin, I got the "#1" middle finger as we left the town square.

I decided to pay a visit to the site of the hit-and-run. I was still trying to wrap my head around why Mr. Parks had been there. Mel went to meet her team to brief them on the events and to assign specific duties.

Apparently, the police had completed their investigation at the scene. The yellow tape was gone. I drove around the building a couple of times for my own peace of mind. I was looking for a beige-colored Chevrolet. The place was deserted. I parked in the back and started to walk around with no idea what I was looking for. After about twenty minutes, finding nothing, I headed back to the office.

When I entered the reception area, Peel pointed to my open office door and put her right index finger to her lips, in the "don't say anything" posture. I nodded. She wrote something on a piece of paper and held it up. It said, "There's someone in your office. She's been waiting for over an hour."

I went into my office, and to my amazement, there sat Mrs. Anne Winfield, the First Lady of Lenore. She looked like someone was holding a gun to her head. I had never seen fear like this in another human being.

"Mrs. Winfield. I'm Brett Simmons. How can I help you?"

Without standing, she offered me her hand. She was trembling.

"Mr. Simmons, I apologize for coming here without an appointment, but I didn't know what else to do."

"No need to apologize, Mrs. Winfield. Can I get you something? Tea, coffee, water?

"Oh, no, thank you, Mr. Simmons. Mrs. Roberts has been very gracious. She gave me some water."

I thought maybe some casual conversation would calm her down. It didn't.

"We call her Peel. It's a long story. And please call me Brett. If I may say so, you appear to be upset."

She was oblivious to what I said. Fear will do that to a person.

"I think I'm next."

I thought I was next.

"Next?" I asked. They tell you in law school that you should never ask a question of a witness, in court, to which you don't already know the answer. In this case, I believed I knew the answer.

"Mr. Simmons, you heard about the accident last night or early this morning? They say it was a hit-and-run."

"I heard. Terrible. It's tragic."

She could barely get the words out. "They're going to kill me next."

"Two questions. May I call you Anne?" She nodded her approval. "Who are 'they,' and why do you think you're next?"

She started to cry.

It took a few minutes but I was able to calm her down. I knew Mel had to be here. I dialed her number.

"Anne, I think it's important that an associate of mine hear what you have to say."

Mel was on her way back to the office. She said her ETA was ten minutes.

It didn't take that long.

CHAPTER 17

AFTER I MADE THE introductions, it was obvious Mel saw what I saw.

Mrs. Winfield—Anne—was a very frightened woman. We could see the terror in her face, in her eyes. Her hands were shaking.

After taking a deep breath, she began, "This is very difficult for me. I'm not used to discussing private things with strangers."

I was glad that Mel was there. In my chosen profession, I'd found that a woman will confide in another woman long before they would to a man, particularly things of an extremely personal nature.

Putting her hand on Anne's shoulder to reassure her, Mel spoke softly: "I know, Anne. It's hard. Just take your time."

"Thank you." Anne paused and took a deep breath. "I've known for a long time that my husband has been having an affair with Dana Parks."

And I had known for a long time as well. It wasn't news to me.

I held up four fingers. Mel nodded. She knew it was Crew Member #4, the grieving widow.

Mel the cop wanted more detail and she took over.

"Does he know that you're aware of his infidelity? Have you confronted him?"

"Yes. He said it was over. He asked me to forgive him. It was the second time I've ever seen him cry."

Mel was trying to be as gentle as she could and wanting to get more familiar with one Warren Winfield. "I'm not trying to be indelicate, Anne. The more information we have, the better we can address the situation. Tell me about the first time he shed tears."

"When he held our newborn daughter. She's twenty-five now and lives in Florida with her boyfriend." Tears were welling up in her eyes.

Mel continued, "Again, Anne, I have to ask this question. Do you think your daughter's in any danger?"

"No. He adores her. He wouldn't let anything happen to her."

Mel pushed a little harder. "I'm sorry, Anne. It's important that I ask you this. Is it over, the affair?"

She smiled that sad smile. "No."

Mel was an experienced interviewer and she knew when to move on.

"So why do you think you're next?"

Anne Winfield was quiet for a moment, putting her thoughts together. "Warren is in over his head. He's involved with some bad people, I mean, *really* bad people." She paused, then blurted out, "They killed Clifford Parks, I know they did!" and began to cry again. "I know too much. Probably not everything, but a lot."

Mel never changed the tone of her voice in the entire interview, questioning and reassuring at the same time. "We have plenty of time, Anne.

You're safe here, and I give you my word that no harm will come to you. Why don't you start at the beginning, I mean, with you and Warren?"

Anne took a sip of her water, then told their story.

"When I met Warren, I fell madly in love him. I was twenty-four and he was twenty-seven. He was so charming. My parents, my family were crazy about him. We dated for about a year and I got pregnant. He did the right thing, as my father used to say, and we got married. I want you to know this: my family is well-to-do. I come from money. Warren did not. He was kicked out of the house by his stepfather when he was eighteen. He went to school at night and got his degree, but he has never really enjoyed financial success on his own. My parents bought our house. They paid for our daughter's education. And several years ago, Warren made some bad investments and we were close to bankruptcy. My parents bailed us out."

Mel pressed on. "Again, Anne, a tough question. Even though he was obviously resentful, do you think he married you for your money, or your family's?"

"I never wanted to believe that. When my grandfather died, I was well taken care of in his will. Let's just say there was a lot of money involved. Warren was so bitter, so angry at the fact that it was my money, my family's money."

Mel sensed that Anne was getting more upset. She pulled the other chair next to her and took her hand. "These are hard questions, Anne. Is this the first time that he's cheated on you . . . that you know of?"

"No. He's had several dalliances, as I call them. But he always came back to me."

Again, Mel changed direction. "So how did Warren meet these bad people?"

"He had just been elected to the town council with Mayor Martin Young."

I interjected, "Anne, I'm the one who got Mayor Young arrested."

Mel said, "I worked on that case as well, Anne."

Anne looked surprised. So was I. I had no idea Mel had been in Lenore before. Then again, I tried to stay an arm's length away from that investigation.

"I was afraid that Warren would get arrested too. He was in on it."

Now it was Mel's turn to look surprised. "I guess we missed that one, Anne."

Anne continued, "I think it was Mayor Young who introduced him to some people at Westlake Industries, one man in particular, a former air force lieutenant colonel."

"Name?" Mel's questions were becoming a little more blunt.

"Karl Jeffords. He and Warren became close friends."

I had heard about him through Judge Jimmy. I couldn't remember what the reference was, but I did recall that Jimmy had spoken about Jeffords in less than glowing terms.

"So where is this Jeffords now, Anne?" I asked.

"On the West Coast. He left Westlake about four years ago. He's now with a company called Pegasus Financial Group."

The hair on the back of my neck stood straight up. Mel shot me a look. Another piece of the puzzle in place.

Anne continued, "Jeffords was a very bitter man. He thought he had been passed over for a promotion in the military because of some vague blemish on his record. Apparently, he left Westlake for the same reason. There was a senior-vice-president position that he thought should've gone to him. It went to a woman. He resigned shortly after that."

Mel picked it back up: "How does your husband fit into this?"

"My husband has told me, on many occasions, that he never wanted to hold public office. It was an opportunity he took that, he thought at the time, could get him closer to his goal. He wanted to be rich, with his own money, not my family's money. His own. He wanted the power that wealth could give him. Karl Jeffords showed him how he could make more money than he ever dreamed of. And Warren jumped in with both feet."

And another of my questions answered. Anne Winfield was filling in a lot of the blanks for me. In this case it was why he didn't pursue a higher goal in his political career.

Mel's interview of Anne Winfield continued.

"Did your husband ever tell you what Jeffords offered him?"

"Not in so many words, at least not at first. Then, a few weeks ago, he told me that things were going ahead as planned. He appeared to be excited. I was concerned that what he was doing was not on the up-and-up."

That got Mel's attention.

"As in illegal?"

Anne nodded. "I think so."

Mel was on a roll.

"Has he been in contact with Jeffords lately?"

"Every day. He went out of town to see Jeffords a few days ago."

I chimed in: "So that's who he went to see with Dana Parks? His trip to the West Coast wasn't on town business?"

She shot me an angry look. She didn't appreciate my reference to Dana Parks traveling with her husband.

She turned to Mel to answer my question. "Yes. He said things were moving very quickly and there were a lot of decisions to be made, but it wasn't his idea to go on that trip."

I thought about my crank call as farmer Sam Dawson.

"What was his demeanor when he returned?" Mel asked.

"I think he was nervous. He would almost jump when his cell phone rang. He didn't like Carlos being around him all the time."

Mel and I both looked at each other. Neither one of us had ever heard this guy's name before

"Who is Carlos?" asked Mel.

"His driver."

So now Rambo officially became Carlos.

"Why does Warren not like Carlos being around him?" I asked.

Anne responded very matter-of-factly, "Carlos works for Pegasus as well. He was sent here as Warren's bodyguard, but I think he was sent to keep an eye on Warren. Although he didn't say it in so many words, Warren thought so too."

Mel wanted to follow this path. "What do you know about Pegasus?"

"I think they're bad people. According to Warren, they have a lot of money. They're buying that property—the Barclay farm. Warren is helping them get the land that those houses sit on, to build the access road to Route 81. There were some other things he's doing for them. I don't know exactly what."

Though unsure if Anne would know, Mel asked anyway, "Did Warren ever say how Pegasus got their money?"

"No, he just said that it had been thoroughly washed. And I heard him talking on the phone. He mentioned the Cayman Islands more than once."

I figured Mel was thinking what I was thinking. Money laundering and offshore bank accounts.

Mel was a pro, no doubt about it. I was learning a great deal from watching her control and steer the interview with Anne Winfield. Her interview technique was like building blocks, one on top of the other. Again she changed directions.

"Did you know Clifford Parks? Had you ever spoken to him?"

"I have met him several times. Social events, that sort of thing. He interviewed me once for a story in the newspaper, but I didn't know him well."

Both Mel and I knew we were getting to a break point. But Mel continued with the questioning.

"When is the last time you spoke to him, Anne?"

"Last night—I mean, before he died—I mean, before he was killed. He called me." She started to cry again. This time she was sobbing.

Mel gave me the time-out sign. I nodded in agreement. Anne Winfield needed a break. So did we.

* * *

Mel and I agreed that Anne Winfield was probably the second-to-last person to talk to the deceased editor/owner. The last was me.

After Peel had made tea, Anne pulled herself together. The fifteen-minute break was a good move on Mel's part. Anne was ready to continue.

Mel picked up where she'd left off.

"Anne, you said that Clifford Parks called you?"

"Yes. Last night. It must have been a little before ten o'clock. Warren got home about ten thirty."

"Were you surprised he called?"

"Yes. Warren and I have cell phones. We don't have a land line. He must have had my number from the time I did that interview with him."

Mel, recognizing that Anne was in a most fragile state, softened her tone. "How did the conversation start, Anne?"

"He apologized for calling so late. Then he blurted out did I know my husband was having an affair with his wife. I said that the affair was over. He said no, it's not over. I felt sick at my stomach."

Tears again.

It took a minute for Anne to regain some semblance of composure. "He said that Warren and his wife were into some bad things with some bad people; that he knew all about what they were doing and how they were doing it, and he was going to expose them—his wife, Warren, and

Pegasus."

I felt like we were beginning to see a little light at the end of this long, dark tunnel.

"He mentioned Pegasus, by name?" I wanted to be sure I'd heard her correctly the first time.

"Yes. He said he knew all about the Barclay property."

"Anne, did he say how he found out?"

"Before I could ask, he said he was a better journalist than people gave him credit for."

Mel's next question would be critical. "Did he say how he was going to expose the operation?"

"He said he was in touch with the authorities. He thought they were on to him, I mean, the bad guys. He told me to be careful and if I needed any help to see Brett Simmons, then he hung up."

Mel and I had exactly the same questions: What authorities? Was he bluffing? Why me? How did I become the last resort?

One thing Anne didn't know and I had to tell her: "Anne, Clifford Parks called me a little after midnight. He wanted to meet me this morning."

She put her hand to her mouth in shock.

Mel knew it was time to wrap it up.

"This has been a harrowing experience for you, Anne. I can't thank you enough for coming forward. It took a lot of courage. I'm going to call one of my agents to pick you up here and take you home to pack some clothes; then you'll go with her to a hotel in King City. She'll stay with you until this is over. If you talk to Warren, tell him that you needed to get away for a few days, nothing more. Now, I'm not trying to alarm you, but I want you to give me your daughter's address in Florida. I'm going to arrange for her to have around-the-clock protection as well. You said your husband would never hurt her, but there's no telling what Pegasus will do."

We were stuck on this merry-go-round. None of what Anne Winfield had told us could be proven in court. Everything Pegasus had done and was continuing to do was all aboveboard. The money laundering: hearsay; the rebuilding of the airstrip: legal; the withdrawal of money by the mayor: not illegal. We had a dead body with no real proof that it was murder.

One of us stayed with Anne until Mel's agent arrived. Literally she never left our sight. We didn't want her to feel abandoned in any way. After Anne Winfield had left with the agent, Mel and I sat down in my office to try to piece all of this together.

"You know, Brett, without Anne Winfield we'd still be in a fog."

"I agree. But along with all this information, we now have more questions."

Mel nodded. "Why you, Brett? Do you think all of your letter writing and emails to Clifford Parks were not in vain after all? To tell Anne Winfield to contact you if she felt in jeopardy, it would seem he trusted you."

I thought about all those letters and emails I wrote and my first meeting with Cliff outside the men's room at the courthouse, which in reality was a confrontation.

"He must have seen something in me, Mel. I thought I had wasted my time. I guess not."

"Do you think he was bluffing about the authorities?"

I knew she was concerned. As I was, to a point.

"I don't get that, Mel. Why would he? Obviously, someone didn't think he was bluffing."

"OK, let's assume he was in contact with some authority or other. If he had contacted our office, I would know. Clay would never leave me hanging."

"The morons in the Lenore Police Department are puppets and Warren Winfield pulls their strings. Can't be them," I said.

We both were thinking the same thing. Mel said it first: "It has to be the feds. Has to be."

Another thing I couldn't shake. My mind kept going back to the Merrifield building. Why was he there? No reason for him to be there between the time he called me and the time they found his body. Maybe he was set up. Maybe he was followed. Maybe we'll never know. Add that to the list of whys.

I'm not sure if I started to think like Mel, or she started to think like me. Probably the former. But we were starting to think alike.

We decided to take another look at the Merrifield building. There had to be something there that we had missed.

And then there was the other elephant in the room. In the back of my mind, as much as it unnerved me, I knew a visit would have to be paid to the Barclay farm. It would seem that if we showed up at the front gate, they weren't going to offer us a free tour of their operation. The situation probably called for a little investigative trespassing. Not sure why I used the pronoun *we*. I had bent the rules too many times already, and certainly trespassing was not in my job description, if I had one. Mel and one of her cohorts could handle those duties. Not sure what they'd find, but it seemed, even after everything Anne Winfield had told us, we were back at the starting gate. It was beginning to feel like we'd never left.

And then there was the mayor's new sidekick. He had a name: Carlos. I had seen a movie about a terrorist from Venezuela in the '70s, Carlos the Jackal. As I recall, a rather nasty, cold-blooded individual. Perhaps, in our current situation, the name was appropriate.

CHAPTER 18

OVER DINNER AT THE Asian Garden, my mind was wandering. Mel took a couple of calls while we ate, giving me some time to mull over all of the day's events. I felt bad for Anne Winfield. If anyone was caught in the middle, it was Anne. And then, of course, there was Clifford Parks. The late Clifford Parks. He was one courageous man, an honest journalist to the end. I had never given either of them much respect and I regretted that.

I had ordered a beer with my meal. Mel advised against it. She asked me to wait until the day was over. I thought it was.

After she had hung up from the first call, she told me that her friend at the tax department had done some checking on our favorite law firm. Clint Davis, the partner who had used his clients' trust accounts as his personal ATM machine, had borrowed the money to repay the debt. After his conviction, the judge gave him three years, suspended sentence, contingent on repayment within eighteen months. He complied with the court order. He would be on probation for an additional eighteen months. The loan had come from a personal friend, one Lt. Col. Karl Jeffords (Ret). Apparently, the colonel had done quite well for himself since leaving Westlake Industries. He had a million and a half bucks sitting around that he could loan to a friend. Mel's associate would do some additional checking. Maybe not all of the Colonel Jeffords' income had been reported on his tax return.

The second call had come from a friend at the Aviation Authority. They did have an airfield registered at the Barclay farm. The registration had been dormant for decades until recently, when the annual fee was paid. The status of the field was listed as unserviceable, which meant that no planes could land there, legally. An additional document had been filed that showed the owner's intent to make the field serviceable again. The paperwork had been submitted by our favorite law firm: Davis, McLean, and Sewell. The check to cover the costs of the filing came from the firm's general account. All wrapped up neat and tidy with a bow and, more importantly, legal. Just a guess, but probably the "firm" recognized that there was no longer any need to conceal their involvement with Pegasus and this land deal thanks to one Brett Simmons.

After I picked up the check in the restaurant and left the tip, we headed for her car.

Wait a minute, why did I pay for dinner?

"I thought you G-people had an unlimited expense account."

"We do." She winked at me, with that grin. "Want to take a little drive, Brett?"

How intuitive of me to think that she wasn't talking about a grand tour of Lenore and its historical sites. Nope.

I saw no point in arguing my case that someone else should be taking a little drive with her.

"Am I riding as shotgun or navigator?"

"Both. We need to stop at your place. The clothes we've got on might not make it through the night."

I wasn't as worried about my clothes making it through the night as I was about me seeing the sun come up again.

Mel didn't have to tell me; I knew we were going to visit the Barclay farm.

I changed into my ninja uniform. Good luck had accompanied me on my last mission, that being the desecration of Sergeant Stuckey's Dodge Caravan, so I decided to wear it again. And there was also the fact that I had nothing else to wear, suitable for the exercise that I was afraid would follow.

Mel came out of the spare bedroom dressed in similar fashion, only she looked way better than me. I had been considering if she qualified. And seeing her in a tight-fitting sweater and even tighter-fitting slacks made my decision easy. I thereby declared—in my head of course—that Melanie Stockton would forever be a DDG. That lifetime designation, being most difficult to achieve, was first declared by one of my law school friends when he described the evening clerk in the law school library, the Blonde Bomber as we called her. After many late-night, and academically unnecessary, visits to said library and careful beer-fueled consideration, there were no dissenting votes; we all agreed with his recommendation.

She was a DDG. And now Mel. She wasn't movie star beautiful, but there was something about her that created a stirring in my loins, similar to the effect that my current main squeeze, Carrie Kincade, had on me. Yep, Melanie Stockton was a DDG. Drop dead gorgeous.

As we headed out from the condo, she asked me, "Do you have a gun?"

I almost swallowed my tongue.

"No. I'm a lawyer, Agent Stockton. The most dangerous thing I own is a letter opener. It's real sharp. It could hurt somebody."

"Well, Counselor, it's not in your best interest to take a knife to a gunfight, or in your case, a letter opener." She laughed. There was something about her laugh. I knew we were in the middle of some serious business, but hearing her laugh made me think she was getting more comfortable with me. My comfort level with Melanie Stockton was growing by the minute.

Then it hit me. A gunfight? What? I wanted to stop right there and think this entire thing over.

She reached in her bag and pulled out a handgun. It was black. That's all I know.

"This is an M&P 9 Shield, the lightest and smallest nine-millimeter personal-defense pistol. This would be used for close-up situations. Here, I'll show you how it works. This little thing here is called a trigger. Pull on this with your index finger and it goes bang."

Again she laughed. I'm not sure what I wanted most: to hear her laugh again or to watch her put this "little" pistol back in her bag.

"Is this really necessary, Agent Stockton?"

"The chances of you actually having to use this are two: slim and none. But we've got a guy—a dead guy—lying in the morgue. We're about to trespass on private property. You tell me."

"I'll probably shoot myself in the foot." I was serious. She was not.

"Or a little higher up. And you'll be singing first soprano with the Berlin Boys Choir. If it makes you feel more confident, soccer moms need about an hour's worth of training to become what they call 'familiar' with this weapon. Lawyers need about a day and a half."

She was grinning again.

Her attempts at making me feel safe and secure failed miserably. All I could do was smile. Not sure if I was more scared of the situation I found myself in or of the cavalier fashion in which my new partner was waving around dangerous firearms. Whatever it was, in a bizarre way, I was starting to enjoy my time with Ms. Melanie Stockton.

And off we went.

There was no direct route from downtown Lenore to the Barclay farm. As my grandfather would say, "You can't get there from here."

We headed east out of town on Church until it became Turner Road. We traveled mostly in an easterly direction for about three miles, until we hit Barclay Side Road. After we turned left, the road meandered west for a few more miles, then north, then east again. I told Mel that we were driving sort of parallel to Route 81. It was not paved, nor had it been repaired lately. Basically, it was a rural road, all bumps and potholes. I was glad my Duster was in the parking garage at the condo. It was slow going and rough. We could only muster about ten miles per hour. And it was dark. We could only see as far as the headlights shone.

Mel was becoming frustrated. "My kingdom for a paved road!" she shouted.

"This is why they wanted those houses, Mel, the eminent domain seizures. There is no direct access to Route 81 from the farm. On the west side, it's Barclay Side Road and we're on it. It turns right, becoming Town Line, going east, at the north end of the property. The east side of the farm is accessible from Boynton Side Road, which eventually merges with Route 81; about a five-mile drive in a northerly direction, on another poorly maintained rural road. They need a direct access from the farm. Our mayor got them the land they needed. Mark my words, Mel, a road will soon appear, from Route 81 to the Barclay farm."

Again her frustration was apparent.

"How much farther, Brett?"

"If my memory is accurate from the chopper ride, we should be coming to a line of what looked like maple trees, delineating the start of the Barclay property."

We both spotted the trees at the same time.

"Pull over, Mel. Let's figure out how we're going to get into the property." We hadn't discussed this little detail. Trespassing on private property was not on my daily to-do list, so I had no idea.

From what Bow Tie had told us, most of the buildings on the farm had fallen into disrepair or collapsed altogether. There was that one building that could be seen from the air; a barn that appeared to be in reasonable shape. We decided to start there, if we could find it in the darkness.

"Among other questions I have, what are we going to do with the car, Mel? We can't leave it here. I'm sure they have security people driving around, keeping an eye on the place."

She tore a piece of paper from her notebook and wrote something on it. She held it up for me to read. "To the police. I ran out of gas. Will return in the morning." She put it under the windshield wiper blade.

"You think you're pretty smart, don't you? Learn that at police school?"

There was that grin again.

"I'll answer that when we get back to your condo, safe and sound."

I wanted to be there already.

The new owners of the Barclay farm had wasted no time locking the place down. As it appeared from the chopper, they had already built a ten-foot-high chain-link fence around the property. What I couldn't see from about a thousand feet up were the five strands of barbed wire at the top. This didn't appear to be your ordinary DIY barbed wire that you can get at your local co-op to keep the cattle from running wild. Nope, this was prison grade. I wasn't sure if they were trying to stop people from getting in or getting out. Maybe both. One thing I was certain about, we'd get cut to pieces trying to scale this fence.

I had climbed over and under all kinds of fence-like obstacles in my youth to help myself to apples, peaches, raspberries—whatever was on the other side. I got a few scratches and bruises, but for the most part, I escaped unscathed. But I never had to negotiate a fence like this, and there was also the fact that I was no longer in my youth. Then I saw it. Although the line of trees was just inside the new fence, there were several low-hanging branches on our side. An obvious oversight on the part of the Pegasus folks.

I pointed them out to Mel. "Are you afraid of heights?"

"Do I have a choice?"

"Sure, if you have a pair of heavy-duty bolt cutters."

"I might have some nail clippers in my overnight bag at your condo. I guess they wouldn't work, huh?"

I just shook my head.

Then again, we didn't want to leave evidence that we had ever been there, and a gaping hole in this brand-new, shiny fence just might be a hint that some uninvited guests had paid a visit to the place.

So after a brief discussion it was decided that the only option open to Agent Stockton and the Ninja Warrior was to get up to the overhanging branches, shinny across, above the fence, and climb down the tree trunk on the other side. Pretty simple and not scary at all. Uh-huh.

Before I could offer myself as the guinea pig and be the first to climb over, Agent Stockton, without saying a word, put her right foot into the fence and raised herself to the lowest limb. She then pulled herself up to the branch that was about three feet above the barbed wire. I couldn't help but notice her athleticism and distinct lack of fear. She shinnied across the branch and over the barbed wire. She climbed down the tree trunk and stood looking at me triumphantly. Although it was dark, very dark, I could see that smug look on her face. She was in and I wasn't.

Another thing I wasn't: I wasn't as nimble as I used to be, or thought I was. I did exactly what Mel did. That was, until I started to shinny across the branch above the barbed wire. They always tell you not to look down. But guess what I did? Yep. Just as I got directly above the fence, I looked down and my left hand slipped off the branch. No, I didn't fall; I was able to catch myself. But there I was, with my butt dangling just inches away from the jagged edges of the barbed wire. Once I regained what little control I had left, I started to move across, hand over hand and leg over leg, basically upside down. The limb started to bounce and I felt it. I had made the acquaintance of the barbed wire. Finally I was able to get to the tree trunk and climb down. It wasn't pretty but now I was in.

"Great job, Counselor. Way to make it look hard." She was being so self-righteous.

I felt around my waistband. No gun.

Again, so arrogantly, she asked, "Looking for something?"

She was holding a little black gun. My little black gun. It must have fallen out during my adventure.

My moment of victory over the barbed wire was short-lived. I felt a tear in the back of my ninja pants. And there was something damp, I mean, wet.

I held my hand up. "I think I cut myself, Mel."

"Are you sure you didn't wet yourself?"

"Very funny. I might be bleeding to death and you're making jokes."

"OK, Ninja Warrior, let's have a look. Drop 'em."

Now, under most circumstances, when an attractive woman asks

Brett Simmons to drop his pants, he complies without hesitation. For some unknown reason, a wave of shyness washed over me.

"Really, Brett! I grew up with a house full of brothers. I might have seen a male tush or two."

So I undid my belt and let my pants fall to my ankles.

Doctor Stockton determined it was a scratch that wouldn't require major surgery. She tore a piece from my already-ripped boxers and wrapped it around my upper leg, or tush as she called it.

"Ninja Warrior ready and able to go back into action," she declared.

I might have been ready and able, but not very willing.

Although it went unsaid, we both understood that there was only one way in and, unfortunately, only one way out, that we knew about. And that was up the tree and over the barbed wire. Maybe there would be an unlocked gate or something and we could simply walk out. Nope, I couldn't get that lucky.

Very quickly two things were brought to my attention: (A) Over the past few months my visits to the gym had become less frequent and I was about to pay a heavy price for that absence; and (B) Agent Stockton was in much better physical condition than I was, on so many levels.

CHAPTER 19

WE COULDN'T USE OUR flashlights. Night-vision goggles, unfortunately, were not in Mel's bag of goodies. We had no idea if there was anyone other than us on the property. We decided to follow the fence line that ran parallel to Barclay Road. It was slow going. We crouched down as we walked. I thought at some point we'd hit the west entrance to the farm and the road that was visible from the air.

I was right. After about thirty minutes we came to the gate. There was a driveway of sorts to our right, heading in an easterly direction. Fighting cramps in our legs, we continued in the crouching position for about ten or fifteen more minutes, and there it was: the barn. It was so dark we almost ran into it. There were no lights, either inside the barn or on the outside. We walked around the perimeter to see if there was an open door or window. We found neither. We had made it to the north side, when out of nowhere there were headlights shining directly at the barn and us. We hit the ground about five feet from the side of the barn. Someone had stopped to unlock the gate. In a few minutes, the vehicle proceeded in our direction.

"Let's hope they don't have a dog," Mel whispered.

My heart hit the roof of my mouth. "*A dog?*" I guess I almost shouted.

"Shhhhh!"

Mel took the gun out of her mini holster on her belt. I took my weapon from my waistband—like I knew what I was doing. My hand was shaking. Even though the evening was cool, I was sweating like a drug dealer in church.

After the vehicle stopped in front of the barn, the driver and a passenger got out. There were two big sliding doors about fifteen feet high. One slid to the right, the other to the left. We could hear both doors opening at once. We could barely hear the men's conversation, but we knew they weren't speaking English. I looked over at Mel and she mouthed the word, "Portuguese." How the hell did she know that?

Once the doors were open the lights inside the barn came on. There was a window right above us and we were fully exposed by the light coming through it. We rolled farther away from the barn, back into the shadows and the long grass.

One of the guys got back into the vehicle and drove it into the barn. The doors remained open.

We lay there in the grass for a few minutes before Mel tapped me on the shoulder. She mouthed the word "quiet," then whispered in my ear, "Hand signals only." The only hand signal I was familiar with was the one where you held up your middle finger displaying your disapproval of something or other. And another thing hit me: in a very short time,

I'd gone from being a lawyer in a comfortable office, to a ninja in the parking lot of the municipal building, and now a Navy SEAL, slithering around on my belly, hiding from two guys speaking a foreign language. How in the wide, wide world of sports did I let myself get into this?

I should be at home watching reruns of *Forensic Files* with my hand firmly wrapped around a cold beer instead of a black handgun that goes bang when you pull the trigger.

I closed my eyes and counted to ten. I have no idea why I did that. It had never worked for me before and it didn't work now.

She tapped my shoulder again, pointed at the window and motioned for me to follow her. We crawled to the side of the barn and stood up with our faces almost touching the outside wall. The window was probably seven or eight feet from the ground. She motioned for me to clasp my hands in the form of a stirrup, which I did. She put her right foot into my hands, and I lifted her up. When she stood up straight her right butt cheek was touching my face. The only thing separating my face from her skin was a razor-thin piece of nylon, or whatever her slacks were made of. If I'd turned slightly to the right, I could have buried my face in her magnificent backside. And don't think for one minute that I hadn't considered doing just that. The combination of whatever perfume she was wearing, the aroma of her slacks, damp from perspiration, and the smell of grass and mud was intoxicating. I honestly felt a little weak in the knees. My interest was not the only thing that was aroused. I needed to get back to thinking with my big head, for the job at hand. As pleasant as this experience was for me, all of her weight was resting on my hands.

I felt like a bodybuilder trying to get that final lift. My entire body started to shake. Finally, she jumped down.

When she turned to me all she whispered was, "Wow."

The courageous part of me wanted to take a look through the window, but the bigger part of me, the sensible part, the one part of my brain that houses the cowardly instinct, wanted to run like hell.

We hugged the side of the barn for what seemed like an hour. It was probably ten minutes. We heard the vehicle start up and back out of the barn. The lights went out. They slid the doors closed and drove down the pathway to the main gate. In a few minutes, after locking the gate behind them, the vehicle turned right, heading north. They would not see the car parked down the road.

Finally, Mel spoke up: "I'd love to get into that building."

I couldn't believe what I'd just heard. "Are you out of your mind?" My question was not rhetorical.

She ignored it. "Do you want to know what I saw?"

"Right now, I want to know how you knew those guys were speaking Portuguese."

"I dated a Portuguese guy once. I can't speak the language, but I recognize it. And it's not Portugal Portuguese. It's South American Portuguese."

"Tomato, tomato!"

Then I remembered that Pegasus was owned by a Brazilian company. Don't they speak Portuguese in Brazil?

"So, what I saw through that window, Brett, will rock your world—

probably the entire world."

"Is there any chance we could talk about this in the relative comfort of my living room? I would like to have this place and this evening squarely in my rearview mirror. Oh, in case you forgot, Agent Stockton, I have a deep laceration on the upper part of my leg, which may require dozens of stitches and plastic surgery. I may have lost a significant amount of blood. As a matter of fact, I am feeling somewhat lightheaded. And even with this serious injury that I have sustained in the name of justice, to get out of here, I still have to climb a tree and shinny across a limb which is situated right on top of the barbed wire, which is how I got this wound in the first place."

I think I may have raised my voice. But Mel was determined.

"No. We're going to try to get into this place. And quit being such a weanie. It's a scratch and it's on your butt, not the upper part of your leg."

I threw my hands up in disgust.

Somehow, the luck of the Irish was on my side, and I'm not even Irish. The barn was locked up tighter than a belt after Thanksgiving dinner.

And wouldn't you know it, whoever was in charge of doling out luck must have figured out I wasn't Irish because it started to rain. Not hard, but just hard enough to make the return trip to our escape egress just that much more difficult. And there was no open gate with a sign that read "Exit." So we headed back from whence we came. By the time we made it back to the tree line, we were wet. Well, I was. Apparently Agent Stockton's outfit was waterproof. Mine wasn't. Thankfully without incident, we repeated the process of climbing the tree to get over the fence. And no, I did not look down.

I had no idea what time it was. It felt like zero dark thirty, or whatever Navy SEALs call it.

"Did you turn your cell phone off before we went in there?"

"What? Why are you asking me that now?"

She was laughing hysterically as we got into the car. Similar to my reaction to her childlike, mischievous grin, I was beginning to enjoy her laugh more each time.

The return ride on Barclay Side Road was no less rough. Funny thing. We did talk on the way back, but not about our most recent experience. There would be time enough for that later on. And guess what Agent Stockton wanted to talk about? How could I forget?

"By the way, Ninja Warrior, you have a nice tush. Very nice."

It took every ounce of strength I could muster to hold back a smile. I didn't want her to have that satisfaction, so I did not respond, hoping we could move on. Nope, she wouldn't let it go.

"I just paid you a compliment, Mr. Simmons. You could say thank you, or something like it."

So I responded, "Thank you, or something like it. Can we talk about something else, anything else?"

She laughed again. This time I smiled.

We drove on for a few minutes, before she started the small talk.

"Did you play any sports, Brett?"

"What do you mean 'did'? I play golf and a little tennis, in the present tense. The little mishap on that tree limb cannot be held against my current level of athleticism."

"Boy, you are touchy tonight, Counselor. Let me rephrase. Did you play sports in school?"

"Yes, I did, in fact. A little football at high school." I was considered small and my contribution to the overall team effort was also small, until my senior year. By then I had acquired some height and girth, and I started every game. I mimicked the PA announcer: "Starting at free safety, number thirty-eight, Brett Simmons."

She jumped in: "Number thirty-eight in the program, number one in our hearts."

"What about you, Mel? Don't answer, let me guess. Basketball?"

She answered with a clearly disgusted tone in her voice. "Why is that every time you see a female over five ten, it's assumed that she played basketball?"

"So it's not basketball?"

"Nope."

"Well, I'm not going to incur the wrath of Ms. Melanie Stockton again by making a wrong guess. You tell me."

"Volleyball."

I admit I didn't expect that. "In high school?"

"Beyond. I played at college. I got a half ride."

"So why law enforcement?"

"Two of my brothers are cops. I majored in criminal justice and psychology. It seemed like a good idea at the time."

"And the other two brothers?"

"My oldest brother is an airline pilot. I'm almost afraid to tell you what the last one does."

"Well?"

"He's a lawyer." She chuckled.

I couldn't help taking a jab at the legal profession. "Underachiever, huh? Probably an embarrassment and a major disappointment for your parents?"

She was laughing. I wanted to hear her laugh more.

"And you, Counselor?"

"My story is very short. I wanted to be Perry Mason."

"That's it?"

"Yep."

"Oh, c'mon, Brett. You can't possibly be serious! Perry Mason—from what, the sixties?—was the major influence in your career choice?"

So I told her about my initial dream to be a doctor and then my lack of success in the natural sciences arena.

She interrupted my story.

"So what kind of doctor would you have been, Brett?"

And of course, the buffoon in me rose to the occasion.

"Well, first of all, Ms. Stockton, I prefer to be called Dr. Simmons. I hardly know you and I'd prefer that we maintain a professional decorum. But for your information, my chosen medical specialty would have been gynecology. What else?"

I wanted to make her laugh again. Nope.

Undaunted, she replied, in a most serious tone, "I would have thought proctology." Then she started to laugh, and in a loud voice announced, "Dr. Brett Simmons, Diseases of the Butt. I guess it wouldn't be a stretch to describe you as being anally retentive."

And we were both laughing. I couldn't help but think of my relationship with Mayor Winfield. I had a hunch she was thinking the same.

"No, really, Brett. Why law? Unless there's some reason you don't want to talk about it."

I hesitated for a few seconds.

"OK, Mel. My mother's brother, my uncle, was a lawyer. I barely knew him. He and my mother were only a year and a half apart in age. They were very close. I guess I was maybe five or six when it happened. He was representing a lady in a very contentious divorce trial. Money and kids involved. Her husband, apparently distraught over the possibility of losing everything, shot and killed his wife, then my uncle, then himself."

She reached over and touched my hand. "Oh, Brett. I'm so sorry."

"Thanks. It was a long time ago. My mother always wanted me to follow in his footsteps. So I did. The end."

Few people knew that story. My parents, of course. My ex-wife, Sarah. Judge Jimmy. And now, Melanie Stockton.

I always felt that my reasons for being a lawyer were deeply personal. And I had always guarded that private part of my life. But I didn't feel uncomfortable in the least opening up to Mel. I knew she appreciated that.

We were a couple of miles from the condo. It was very quiet in the car. We were both tired and glad that our adventure was almost over.

She broke the silence.

"Brett, have you ever thought about quitting, doing something other than being a lawyer?

That had never crossed my mind.

"No, not at all. Oh sure, I would give up my practice if a judgeship was ever tossed my way, like that's ever gonna happen. And you? Have you ever thought about handing in your badge?"

I thought, having seen her in action less than an hour ago, that it was a dumb question. It wasn't.

There was a serious tone in her answer. "Yes."

I didn't pursue it any further as we turned into the entrance to the condo. I knew if she wanted me to know the details, she would tell me.

It was a little after midnight.

If she wanted to tell me, I would have liked to hear about her wanting to leave law enforcement, but considering what we had just experienced, I did want to know what she'd seen through that barn window. I really did. But first, I wanted to lose the Ninja Warrior getup, check on the severity of my injury, take a hot shower, and place my hands around a cold beverage. And not necessarily in that order.

CHAPTER 20

HAVING SHOWERED AND ALSO having awkwardly checked my tush in the mirror, I discovered that Dr. Stockton's initial diagnosis regarding the severity of my injury was correct. It wasn't much more than a scratch. A little Polysporin and I was on my way to a complete recovery.

Mel had also taken advantage of a hot shower. I know she was bursting at the seams to tell me about what she'd seen in the barn. We were in the living room. She had accepted my offer of a cold beverage. I was trying to relax and she was at the other end of the spectrum. I could never have imagined her being this animated. But in describing what she'd seen inside the barn, she couldn't sit down; her hands were flailing all over the place; her voice was almost at a soprano level. She was like a ten-year-old girl getting her first Barbie doll for Christmas.

"I really wanted to get inside that barn, Brett."

"Maybe it's the lawyer in me, or maybe the coward, but I was OK with us not getting into the barn. Do you want me to list all the laws we broke this evening?"

She ignored me and carried on.

"First, let me say you're welcome," she eventually replied.

"For what?"

"Remember that late-model Chevrolet that tried to run you off the road? Well, I found it."

"Are you serious?"

"Yep, it was sitting on a trailer, ready to be towed to who knows where. And more importantly, there was some damage to the passenger-side headlight. Pretty significant. Could it have come from his ramming into you?"

I shook my head.

"I don't think so. It was bumper to bumper. I don't think the headlight made contact with my car."

"Brett, I really wanted to get in there to see if there was any blood around the damage."

"From Clifford Parks?"

"Uh-huh. From how you described him, I believe the tall, dark-headed one was Carlos the Jackal. The other guy was short and squat. And there were lots of other goodies. The barn is huge, larger than it looks from the outside, and the inside has had a significant makeover. You'd expect to find a dirt floor in a barn like that. At least half of it is concrete, probably newly poured. There were four stainless-steel tables, about ten feet long, lined up parallel to one another. Boxes, maybe twenty or so, were stacked up on the tables. I could make out the writing on a couple of the boxes. Greenway Sod Farm. Not sure what that is. And someone has drywalled most of the interior, the far wall for sure. There was a desk and several tables with computers and printers. So you see why I wanted to get into that barn. I was hoping that Carlos and his pal would have left us a way to get in after they drove off. No such luck."

"Yep. Sorry for being such a weanie, Mel, but I was not comfortable in that place."

"I wasn't either. But I'm glad we did it. I mean, going there. Thanks. No way I could have done that by myself."

I nodded. "Did any of that stuff look like something a sod farm would use?"

"I know diddly-squat about farming, Brett, sod or otherwise, but it's reasonable to assume that growing sod doesn't require shiny tables. I'm intrigued by those boxes. It was hard to tell if they were coming or going."

She took a couple of sips from her beer. No glass, right out of the can. Then she got surprisingly quiet, zoning out. Her eyes became glossy.

"Penny for your thoughts, Mel."

It took her a few moments to respond.

"I was just thinking about your uncle. How tragic, Brett. I mean, you could have practiced law with him."

"I know. I often think about that. When I visit my parents, I can count on my mother bringing it up. She misses him more than I can imagine."

"I feel so sorry for her. Maybe one day I can tell her."

"She'd like that, Mel. So would I."

She got very quiet again. Then she stared at me for a moment or two with a sad look on her face. Then it came, pouring out of her: "The guy I shot . . . why I had to take a leave." Her voice started to crack. "I took him out. I killed him, Brett."

She looked down at the beer can she was holding. I could tell she was fighting the tears. I wasn't sure what to do or what to say.

"You don't have to, Mel. You don't have to talk about it. I know it's painful."

"But I do have to. I have to tell you."

She continued, "There had been an incident in a small town up near Elkhart. A convicted felon on parole had been arrested for illegal firearm possession. He knew he'd end up back in prison to finish out his sentence, plus more time for the weapon's charge. So he busted out of the local jail, with his girlfriend's help. Clay sent me up there to assist in the investigation of how this guy got out and maybe to assist in his recapture."

She took a deep breath and continued.

"They were able to arrest his girlfriend and eventually she told them that he was holed up in an abandoned farmhouse. I accompanied the local cops to the location. We surrounded the place and waited on the SWAT team to arrive. The perp was aware of our presence. The local guys had a bullhorn and they were attempting to negotiate with him to surrender. He refused to talk. I suspected what he had in mind was suicide by cop. Anyway, in the heat of the moment one of the cops decided to move to a better location. He stood up and the guy in the farmhouse shot him."

I guess my mouth was hanging open. They can't make this stuff up, even in Hollywood.

"The cop just lay there, moaning. We couldn't get to him. He was right in the open."

"Where were you?" I thought, Probably right in the middle of things.

"I had made them aware of my marksmanship skills, so they had me climb up to the hayloft in the barn. From my vantage point I had a clear view of the farmhouse. I always carry my Remington 700 rifle with me."

The only "Remington" I was familiar with was the electric shaver my dad once owned. Apparently, they make rifles as well.

Her eyes were closed as if she was recreating the entire scene in her head.

"I felt so helpless. We all did. We had to get that officer to the hospital and fast."

She took another deep breath.

"We knew that the escapee was wearing a blue Colts wool cap. I saw him raise his head in one of the windows. I knew it was him. According to what his girlfriend had told us, he was the only one in the farmhouse. I waited for what seemed like forever. I was ready. Then he raised his head again and I fired."

She continued to stare at the beer can. There was an awkward silence. I wanted to give her a hug, hold her hand—something. I wasn't sure if she had finished her story.

"Did the officer make it, Mel?"

She looked up. A smile crept over her face. A good sign. "Yes, thank goodness."

Then she became fixated on the beer can again. "I didn't want to kill him, Brett. That gun and the ammunition . . . it blew half of his head off. I've never killed anyone in my life. And that's why I considered handing in my badge."

I didn't want to sound patronizing but I had to say something.

"But you didn't. I mean, resign. You had to shoot this guy. No other choice. But you probably saved the officer's life. I'm guessing he would have died if he had lain there much longer."

She looked up at me again. "I know. I have to keep telling myself that."

I wanted to get her mind off the shooting.

"How is the officer now?"

"I'm in contact with the chief of police up there. I talked to him the other day, you know, just checking on the officer. It's better. But he faces a long road of surgeries and rehabilitation. He'll never go back to his job. Ever. But at the very least, his family has him. And I am glad I could help."

I responded, again, without thinking, but I had to say it: "Help? You saved his life. And having known you for only a short time, to save someone else, even a small-town lawyer, push comes to shove, you'd do it again."

She just nodded. And that, in my opinion—and I haven't changed my mind—is why she continued to carry the badge.

She looked right into my eyes. "Brett . . . thanks for letting me unload on you."

"No worries. What are friends for?"

"I know."

It was time to move on. We'd had a long day. A rough one. And I had no idea what the next day would hold for us.

I felt she was ready for my question. "I may regret asking this, but what's next?"

Yep, she had another devious plan up her sleeve.

"Are you up for making an anonymous call, Counselor?"

"Will I be breaking the law again?"

"Let's just say you'll be a concerned citizen doing his civic duty."

"I can hardly wait."

On that note we decided to get some sleep. I guess at some point I drifted off, but not before I thought about Melanie, the injured officer, and the dead guy; about what I would do if I wasn't a lawyer; and about my uncle and what it would have been like to practice law with him. Surprisingly, even though I had a lot swimming in my mind, I didn't have to dip into my supply of melatonin.

* * *

The next morning, I called David, Brad, and Bow Tie to see if any of them had heard of Greenway Sod Farm. They had not. Bow Tie said he'd do some digging to see if a business license had been issued to this company, and over coffee and a danish at the Shack, Mel shared her plan with me.

* * *

We drove over to the house that Jimmy and his son-in-law had owned. Eminent domain had run its course. They had been recently evicted, along with all the other homeowners, but we were sure demolition had not yet started. Mel knew that if we parked at the rear of the property, with field glasses, we could see the front of the barn on the old Barclay place.

Once we had parked, she handed me her phone. I dialed Chief Pryor's direct line.

"Pryor here."

"Chief. I have some information regarding the hit-and-run accident."

"Who is this?"

"Do you want the information or not?"

"Of course."

"There's a barn on the old Barclay place. The car involved, a late-model Chevrolet, is sitting in there. Take some bolt cutters and your forensic guys with you. You'll find plenty of evidence."

Then I hung up.

Mel was looking at me. "Do they have a forensic unit in Lenore?"

"Not to my knowledge."

She just shook her head.

Now we waited. It took about ninety minutes for the show to begin. A pickup truck with dual rear tires pulled up to the gate. Our friend Carlos the Jackal got out and opened it. He got back in and drove up to the barn. We could see he had a passenger. After they opened the large doors, he backed the truck inside. A few minutes later the truck pulled out with the trailer attached. On the trailer was the Chevrolet. They had put a dustcover over the car, hiding the damaged front end, but we knew what it was.

I was sure that he would take Barclay Side Road to Town Line over to Boynton Road, then head north, which would eventually take him to the junction with Route 81. We would wait there and follow him to see where he was taking the car.

We were already on Route 81, so we were able to get to the exit well before Carlos.

When he got to the intersection, as expected, he turned north toward King City. We were able to stay well behind. A pickup truck hauling a car trailer wouldn't be easily lost in heavy traffic.

Route 81 becomes Treadwell Road just as you enter the King City limits, named after Ross Treadwell a World War II B-17 pilot credited with saving his airplane and crew after they were strafed by German fighters. He later died from the injuries he received in that action. Lieutenant Treadwell would not be happy with what his namesake road had become. Let's just say the southern part of King City was now the seedier part of town, with pawn shops, strip clubs, used-car lots, body shops, and motels renting rooms by the hour. Carlos turned the pickup and trailer into one of those businesses. "Reliable Auto Repair, George Kostopoulas, Proprietor," so the sign read. We parked just down the street. We had to wait about thirty minutes for Carlos and his friend to re-emerge from behind the building. The trailer was empty.

We got out of the car and as we were entering the front door of Reliable Auto Repair, Mel whispered, "This is my favorite part of the job."

* * *

Behind the desk sat a rather portly gentleman wearing blue overalls that hadn't been near a washer in quite some time. Underneath the straps was a dirty, grease-stained T-shirt that had once been white. He had curly salt-and-pepper hair. His rather bushy eyebrows matched the hair. Stuck in his red-cheeked, chubby face was a well-chewed, unlit cigar. He was fully engrossed in the horse racing section of the *King City Daily News*. He didn't lift his head as we approached his desk, he just raised his eyes over the newspaper.

It was Mel that started the repartee.

"You George?"

"Who wants to know?"

She took her badge out of her jacket pocket and held it out. "Melanie Stockton. Special Agent, Investigative Services, Attorney General's Office."

The man put down his paper, stood up, and walked over to look at the badge.

"As soon as you stop staring at my breasts, would you mind taking a quick look at the badge?"

I can remember being told by my high school football coach that I needed to "grow a pair." This lady would not have to be so advised.

"So again, are you George?"

"All my life."

"George, this is my associate Brian Timmons."

I shot a quick, icy look in Mel's direction. Now I'm impersonating a cop.

"What can I do for you, little lady?"

I knew this wasn't going to end well for George.

"Did a gentleman just bring a beige Chevrolet in here with a busted front headlight?"

He shrugged his shoulders. "Could have. I really don't know."

"Are you going to repair it or sell it for parts?"

Again, that I-don't-know-anything-about-that look. "What car are you talking about?"

"Do you know what 'obstruction' means, George? I'm sure a man of the world like yourself is familiar with that term. We're conducting an official investigation here. I need to take a look at that car."

"You'll need a search warrant, Ms. Stocker."

She ignored the mispronunciation of her name. "Can do, George, but in the meantime . . ." Mel took her cell phone out of her pocket. "See this here phone, George. I'm going to place a call to Captain Morris of the King City Police Department's Criminal Investigation Division. He's an old pal who owes me a favor. I'm going to tell him that we suspect you're running a chop shop at this establishment. He's going to come down here with a search warrant and about twenty officers and tear this place apart, and if there's one—just one—vehicle on your lot without a registration, your Greek ass is going to jail. Ball's in your court,

George. What's it gonna be? My way or the hard way?"

He reached around and took a set of keys from a hook on a pegboard and tossed them to Mel. "Car's out back."

"Your cooperation is much appreciated, George."

As we walked through the back door, she turned back and said, "Oh, and by the way, George, if I find out that you've alerted the fellow with the heavy accent who just brought that car here, you'll wish you had been arrested by Captain Morris and his band of King City Police Officers. Understand?"

George nodded.

We found the car probably where Carlos had left it.

Mel was focused and meticulous. She put on a pair of latex gloves. I just stood back and observed. With her phone, she photographed the license plate, the damage to the headlight, the marks on the front bumper more than likely from my car, and the tire treads.

She turned to me and said, "Hopefully, our lab folks will get some prints off the steering wheel. Our friend, Carlos, was not wearing gloves that I could see. He had to back it down off the trailer."

I hadn't noticed either way.

Around the damaged headlight area, there were some specks. "Probably blood," she said. More pics with her phone.

She thoroughly searched the trunk, the glove compartment, and the inside of the car, front and back. It appeared as though someone had taken the time to clean those areas.

When we were finished, Mel took the keys back to George.

"Thanks, George. I'll advise Captain Morris of your cooperation. Having a guy like him on your side is a good thing, George. Oh, and one other thing. Don't touch that car. Got it?"

George nodded his understanding.

As we headed for the car, Mel started laughing. That laugh again.

"Sometimes, Brett, I love my job!"

"I have to ask. Do you know a Captain Morris of the King City Police Department?"

"Who?"

I shook my head.

"As much as it pains me to say it, that was an Academy Award performance in there. Do you think George will do something with the car?"

"Brett, you mean something stupid? I doubt it. What I have discovered, over the years, is that when people who have something to hide, and I'm sure our Greek friend does, they will give you the keys to their kingdom to avoid having anyone take a closer look behind the curtain."

"So that's why he let us look at the Chevy, so we don't look at anything else."

"You are correct, sir."

"And what is my alter ego, Timmons or something? I think that's impersonating a police officer, and if I learned anything over the years, that's illegal."

"Whatever."

As soon as we reached the car, she tossed me the keys. "You drive, I have to make some calls. I have to order a search-and-seize warrant.

I want that car impounded. I think George will cooperate, don't you?"

I had just maneuvered into traffic, heading south, when Mel turned to me and said, "How strong is a chain?"

I hesitated for a moment, trying to figure where she was going with this.

"You see, Brett, you think like a lawyer, trying to get people off. Innocent, not guilty. Me, on the other hand, I'm trying to put guys in jail. Answer the question."

Quoting my grandfather, "A chain is only as strong as its weakest link."

"Correct. And who is the weakest link in the Pegasus chain?"

I didn't want to appear stupid, so I didn't answer the question. "You're about to tell me."

"Your friend and mine, Carlos the Jackal."

"Why him?"

"He's not that smart. Case in point: all the evidence I believe he left behind on that Chevy. And for him it'll be all about self-preservation. When given a choice of saving his own butt or protecting his employers, which way do you think he'll go?"

I was about to answer when she started dialing her phone.

Our next stop would be the Merrifield building. I wanted to have one more look around. Clifford Parks went there for a reason. I had as much a reason for going back there. It's the least I could do for the late owner/editor.

CHAPTER 21

MEL MADE ARRANGEMENTS TO get a warrant to impound the Chevrolet. She also asked her people to do some research on Carlos the Jackal. We didn't have a last name, but we knew that he worked for Pegasus. She called one of her associates in Lenore and told them to get ready to head over to George the Greek's place to impound the car and wait on the forensics team.

She had put the phone back in her pocket when she started to chuckle.

"I don't trust the lab in Lenore."

I laughed. "Yep, if we had one."

"Twenty bucks, Brett."

"What?"

"I'll bet you twenty bucks that Carlos is not a citizen of our great country and he fibbed a little on his Visa application, like maybe his real name, and whether or not he's ever been charged with a felony somewhere in the world."

I shook my head. "Nope. I'm not going to add to the nine thousand dollars you hypothetically took from your bank account."

She smiled. "Just like Clay. So smug with your sense of humor."

We didn't talk much after that, until we pulled into the vacant parking lot behind the old Merrifield building.

"Can I ask what you're looking for, Brett? I thought you did a pretty good sweep of the place before."

"I did. But I still can't figure out why he came here several hours before our meeting."

"I'm thinking that whatever he brought here—if anything—is now in the hands of Pegasus."

"That's what I'm afraid of, Mel. But I want to have another look."

Mel started on one side and I took the other. The doors were secure, and the windows had been covered up with plywood. There was no way to get into the building without a crowbar. Eventually we worked our way around and met at the perimeter of the pavement, where the grass and shrubbery were overgrown, making the search that much more difficult. Finally, after about twenty-five minutes, I threw my hands up.

"Nothing, Mel. Nothing." I was frustrated.

For whatever reason, I found myself staring at it. A mailbox, perched on a weathered four-by-four post leaning precariously toward the road. What had once been a shiny, black metal tube was now rusty and barely upright. I don't know whose mailbox it was, but I walked over to take a look. The small door was wedged in place, with only one hinge holding it on. I struggled to pull it open, but when I did it was empty, or so I thought. Now I'm not one to go sticking my hand into places that might be inhabited by spiders or ants or some other crawling insects that bite, but for some reason I reached in and I felt something. It was a small plastic baggie. I felt my knees grow weak. My mouth went dry. My heart started to pound out of my chest as I pulled it out and saw a USB flash drive looking back at me. What would something like that be doing in a place like this? There was only one answer.

I said a quiet thank-you to the editor/owner: "We'll take it from here, Clifford. You can rest in peace."

* * *

Mel drove back to the condo. I couldn't get Clifford off my mind. I wished I could have known him, under different circumstances, of course. I'm sure we would have hit it off. We had a lot in common: our love for Lenore and the tenacity with which we both upheld our personal integrity. I was sure our moral compasses were set on the same heading. I didn't have any idea what we'd find on that flash drive I was holding, but whatever it was, I suspected it had cost Clifford his life.

As we pulled into my parking spot in the underground garage, Mel took out her gun. I guess I looked surprised.

"These people probably killed Clifford Parks for what you're carrying. They wouldn't hesitate for a moment to kill you and me. Let's be cautious. Better safe than sorry."

"Do you think anyone saw us over at the Merrifield building?"

"Hard to tell, Brett. I think if that were the case, they would have confronted us there. Let's hope they don't know we've got it."

It was a quiet ride in the elevator up to the fourth floor.

Once inside the condo, she made a quick sweep of every room. Clear. At least I thought.

She mouthed to me, "Talk normal, don't mention the baggie."

I nodded.

In a louder than normal voice, she said, "I'm going to take a shower. You said you had a headache. Why don't you lie down for a while before we head out to dinner?"

"Good idea," I replied, trying to figure why she was going through this exercise.

She motioned for me to follow her into the bathroom. She turned the water on in the sink, then lowered the lid and sat down on the toilet. She pointed to the edge of the tub. I sat down clutching the flash drive.

She spoke softly. "Someone's been in here, Brett. I always leave my suitcase on the floor, top side facing the door. It's backwards. Someone moved it. Do you have a cleaning service?"

"I do, but they come on Fridays, not today."

"The place may be bugged. Typically, they wouldn't put a microphone in the bathroom. I think we're OK in here."

I was glad she was confident. I wouldn't know a "bug" if I had one in my hand. She's good, I thought. A real pro.

"I'm actually glad they did this. It confirms so much of what we suspect. If there's a bug in here anywhere, we'll leave it alone. We want them to think that they're one step ahead of us. Does your office have a security system?"

"Yes. An alarm with a motion detector. I'm not saying it's foolproof, but it's better than nothing, which is evident in how secure my condo is."

"Can we go there and take a look at the flash drive? I don't want to do it here."

"Sure."

After a few more minutes of play acting, we headed out to my office, with guns at the ready. Well, Mel's was.

CHAPTER 22

ON THE SHORT RIDE over to the office I made a mental note to contact the security folks to have a system installed at the condo. I didn't care much for the fact that someone had paid a visit to my place of refuge without an invitation. Nope, not happy.

"Gotta get me a security system for the condo, Mel."

"Good idea, Counselor, other than the fact that the horse has already left the barn, and if you install a system now, the bad guys might surmise that you know they've been there. I thought we agreed we didn't want that to happen. Maybe after this whole thing, whatever it is, has reached its natural conclusion."

"You're right, Mel. You think like a cop and I think like a lawyer."

As we got close to the office, Mel added to my unstable frame of mind.

"It's almost seven o'clock, Brett. Everything should be shut down by now. I'm going to do a drive-by to see if there's any suspicious vehicles lurking about, keeping an eye on the place."

I turned around and looked through the rear window to see if we were being followed. Bad idea, according to Mel.

"Countersurveillance One Oh One, Brett. Never turn around and check to see if you're being followed. We have these handy mirrors. They work really well. And no, I've been checking, we're not being followed. They probably installed those bugs in the condo hoping we would be in for the night and there wouldn't be a need to follow us."

"I'm getting tired of you being right and then you lecturing me like I'm a fifth-grader."

"Sucks to be you, Counselor. Actually I was lecturing you like a third-grader." She laughed. I didn't.

We made a pass in front of the office. I didn't see anything out of the ordinary. She turned right onto Murray Street, then another right onto Berry Road, which goes directly past the rear of my office building. Again, nothing strange. The parking lot was well lit, with only a white van parked close to the rear door.

"That van belongs to the office cleaning crew, Mel."

"Good. That means business as usual. Let's park here and go in the back way."

I disengaged the alarm system after we had entered the office. Peel had armed it a little after five as she was leaving. The monitor indicated no one had entered or left the office between then and the cleaning company's arrival. Everything appeared to be normal.

We went directly to my office, and after closing the door, I turned on my laptop and plugged in the flash drive. It took a few seconds before anything appeared on the screen. Exactly what I was afraid of: it asked for a password. I turned to Mel with that "what are we supposed to do now?" look. She shrugged.

Then I remembered the last thing Clifford Parks had said to me before he hung up.

"Mel, Clifford Parks said the key word is 'fact.' Maybe he meant password."

I slowly typed it into the space and hit enter. Nope. Denied.

So I keyed in the numbers that corresponded to the letters on a phone.

Bingo. We were in.

Mel, standing behind me, leaned in to get a better look at the screen and put her hand on my left shoulder. She didn't seem to be one of those touchy-feely people, so I assumed she was getting as comfortable with me as I was with her. I didn't mind it. Not one bit.

What came up was a note to me:

Mr. Simmons,

You may know, or at least suspect, that something sinister is happening at the old Barclay farm. What I'm about to tell you is highly classified, and the only reason I am sharing this information with you is that I believe my situation is precarious, at best. I have been working undercover for the federal government. More specifically, for a combined task force comprised of several law enforcement agencies in what they are calling Operation Rio, as in Rio de Janeiro. They are investigating Pegasus, among other so-called legitimate business-es based in Brazil.

I have been under suspicion by Pegasus ever since Carlos got here. I wanted to meet with you to let you know that they tried to hack into my laptop and my cell phone last night. I don't believe they were successful. I am writing this on a spare desktop at the Gazette.

They are aware that it was you who placed the call to Davis, McLean, and Sewell and left the voicemail on the Pegasus line.

This may come as a surprise, Mr. Simmons, but you are my in-surance policy. I know I can trust you. Should something happen to me, and if you're reading this, then it probably has, please contact Paul Gallagher at 202-555-0137. It's his direct line. He's aware that I may be in some jeopardy.

Karl Jeffords is dirty. Warren Winfield is dirty. And it's with a broken heart that I tell you my wife, Dana, is dirty. No matter what she has done, including betraying me and our marriage, I still love her. Strange, isn't it?

Above all else, Mr. Simmons, please be careful. These people are ruthless.

It was eerie reading Clifford Parks's note. It was like he was writing to an old friend. And it was like he was predicting his own demise.

It seemed several minutes went by before either Mel or I could speak.

I was struggling to understand. "I would never had guessed that Clifford Parks had it in him . . . I mean, to do something like this."

"Me neither, Brett. We need to make that call. Or, more specifically, *you* need to make that call."

I dialed the number Clifford Parks had given us and hit speaker. I wanted Mel to hear everything.

One ring. Two rings. Three. Four. Then he picked up.

The voice was gruff, short and to the point. "Talk to me."

"Mr. Gallagher, my name is Brett Simmons. I'm a lawyer in Lenore."

"How'd you get this number?" He was obviously not happy that I'd called.

"From Clifford Parks. I don't know exactly how to say this, but he's dead."

"What? If this is some kind of joke, pal—"

"No joke, Mr. Gallagher. Struck by a car. Hit-and-run."

There was a pause. I'm certain he was assessing the situation. He had to make sure I was legitimate. "How do I know you are who you say you are?"

"We know about Operation Rio."

That got his attention. He was barking into the phone: "What do you mean 'we'—who else knows?"

"Melanie Stockton. She's a special investigator in our attorney general's office. She's standing right beside me."

"Where are you right now?"

"In my office."

"Stay right where you are. I'll be there in about three hours." Then he hung up.

I turned to Mel. "He never asked for an address or directions or anything."

"If he's a fed, he already knows or he can quickly find out."

The clock on my laptop said it was almost seven thirty.

Mel headed for the small office kitchen.

"Got anything to eat in this place? If we have to wait for three hours for this guy, I would like to do so on a full stomach."

It had been a long time since breakfast. Thankfully, Peel kept the refrigerator well stocked, but I wasn't sure if I was more tired than hungry.

The day—as eventful as it had been—was far from over.

CHAPTER 23

AT 10:48 P.M. MY cell buzzed. A text: "ETA, 20 min. Gallagher."

It had been the longest three hours plus of my life. Mel and I did get some food into us. Thank you, Peel.

Twenty minutes later, another text: "In the parking lot, open up. Gallagher."

Apparently this guy was not one to waste words. At least not on me.

I went to the back door of the building and opened it. There were three of them exiting a black SUV. They had parked a few spaces away from Mel's car. The cleaners and their van were long gone.

I wasn't sure where they came from or how they got here. I was convinced that they wouldn't tell me anyway.

All three were dressed in black suits, white shirts, and black ties. Triplets. Well, not exactly. The two younger guys were taller, with muscles bulging out of their well-tailored suit coats. The third guy, the older one, was considerably shorter and apparently the leader. It was obvious, regardless of his age, that the years had not been kind to him. He had lines deeply etched into his forehead. The heavy jowls were not his most distinguishing feature; it was the enormous bags under his eyes. Sleep was probably an indulgence seldom experienced. His suit, in contrast to the two younger gentlemen's, hadn't seen the inside of a dry-cleaning establishment in quite some time. As he walked up to me, I was expecting a handshake. None was forthcoming.

"Gallagher."

"Brett Simmons."

I showed them into my office, and I locked the door.

"Mr. Gallagher, this is Melanie Stockton."

Gallagher nodded. No handshakes. Social graces were not on his agenda.

"My associates, Mr. Bannister and Mr. Pruitt. Whatever you have to say to me, you can say to them. Understood?"

As badges were shown, Mel and I nodded in unison. I was the only one who was badge-less.

Gallagher was in charge and wasting no time, and he wanted us to be aware of that fact.

"Before we move forward with any discussion, I need you to sign a document. It's part of the Secrecy Act. No need to read it. Just sign it."

One of his associates had already taken the papers out of a briefcase.

And like so many other times, my mouth reacted first. I guess it was the lawyer in me coming out.

"Mr. Gallagher, I'm a lawyer. I don't sign anything before I read it."

He dismissed me in short order. "Mr. Simmons. I have neither the time nor the legal necessity to fool with you. Sign it now or I will place you under arrest. Pick one."

I guessed that my legal rights, and those of Mel, had no standing with Mr. Gallagher, in this situation. Aware that he wasn't kidding, I looked at Mel. She signed the document. I followed suit.

"Alright, folks, let's get started."

I pointed to the conference room. Gallagher nodded his approval.

Once we were seated, one of the twins—as I started to call them in my mind—pushed the red button on a digital recording device that he removed from the aforementioned briefcase. He nodded to Mr. Gallagher, and then I got the fickle finger of fate.

"You're up, Mr. Simmons. I need to know what you know—and how you know it. From the beginning, if you don't mind. Be patient, Ms. Stockton. You're next."

I took them, as thoroughly as I could, through all the bends and curves in the story. Gallagher listened intently and took notes without interrupting me even once. When I finally came to the late-night call from Clifford Parks, he held up his hand with a "stop right here" gesture.

"Before you continue, I want to make sure I understand who the players are."

He referred to his notes.

"So, along with Agent Bonner, there's you two, a David Spencer, a Brad Perryman, and a guy you call Bow Tie. And these last three gentlemen are members of the town council, correct?"

"Correct. David and Brad are both married. I'm not sure how much their spouses know."

"And they do not know about Operation Rio?"

"Correct. They have no knowledge of Operation Rio."

Gallagher motioned for me to continue.

I finished with our finding the flash drive and then reading it before I placed my call to him. I had printed a copy of Clifford Parks's message. I handed it to him.

Then it was Mel's turn. She outlined what she knew and then listed the contacts in the various agencies she had involved in his investigation, as well as the location of Anne Winfield and her daughter.

When she was finished, Gallagher looked at his notes and then shared his conclusions.

"From where I'm sitting, I don't think our operation has been compromised, although that doesn't mean there's an absence of concern on my part. Cliff didn't think they were able to hack his laptop and his phone. Do we know where those devices are right now?"

Mel and I shook our heads.

"We'll break for a few minutes, then it's my turn. Any coffee in this place, Mr. Simmons?"

"In the kitchen," I responded. "And if you're hungry, there's some sandwich stuff in the fridge."

I think I detected a faint smile from Mr. Gallagher. I could have been mistaken. He pointed to the kitchen. "Great. Mr. Bannister, would you do the honors?"

After about twenty-five minutes, we reconvened in the conference room. It was heading for midnight.

Gallagher wasn't about to let us forget who was in charge. "Before I start, folks, may I remind you that you have both placed your legal signatures on a document verifying your secrecy regarding what I'm about to tell you. Understood?"

Again, in unison, Mel and I nodded our understanding. Our newest friend—that being Mr. Gallagher—although diminutive in stature compared to his two traveling companions, could command a room. When he spoke, people listened. We did.

"I don't think I need to outline the punishment for failure to observe the Secrecy Act, to the letter.

After a short pause, he cleared his throat and began. The recording device had not been activated.

"My name is Paul Gallagher. And like you, Mr. Simmons, I'm a lawyer. And like you, Ms. Stockton, I'm a cop—well, formerly. So we do have some things in common. I won't bore you with the details of how I find myself in this position, but suffice it to say, I am second-in-command of a major combined federal task force conducting a C and C operation that you now know is code-named Rio."

And in situations like this, right about now—and you know me pretty well—the buffoon in me, first identified by my ex-wife, Sarah, made an appearance. I started thinking about how James Bond would handle this. Some might argue that it must be fatigue or maybe some kind of chemical imbalance that makes me do it. In reality, it's these brief visits to Crazyville that keep me from losing my mind.

I had no idea what "C and C" meant. I was about to find out.

"Folks, this task force was created by certain government officials at the highest level, some two years ago. Now don't be fooled by the start date. We have been investigating these criminals for many years, but as individual agencies, acting independently of each another. Now we are acting as one."

I took notice of the fact that he labeled these people, whoever they were, as criminals.

Gallagher continued, "This team, Operation Rio, on paper, does not exist. Only those directly involved have knowledge of its existence. We are financed by a classified discretionary fund only available to those same high-level government officials. As such, every action taken is done so C and C, covert and clandestine."

Two things hit me: (1) Now I know what C and C is. (2) He referred to "government officials at the highest level." Could one of those officials occupy a desk in the Oval Office? At this point, nothing would have surprised me.

He went on with his background explanation. "You may ask, Why the secrecy? Good question. Our team not only consists of our national agencies, but we have been joined by similar agencies in other countries, specifically in South America, whose members would be in grave danger should this operation be discovered. Also, the bad guys would close up shop and hunker down for as long as it takes to restructure and reorganize, which would cause all of our efforts over the past two years to have been a total waste of time and assets. Until we can be certain of our success, this undertaking has to remain secret. So you see why we had to get you to sign those documents."

Now it was starting to make sense. I glanced over at Mel. She was locked in.

"Our target: O Grupo dos Seis, which is Portuguese for 'The Group of Six.' They are the bad guys. And when I say bad, there are no words in the English language to adequately describe the depths of evil to which they routinely stoop to achieve their ends."

Add my friend Carlos the Jackal to that group.

"The Group of Six are not individuals. They are six families, located mostly in Brazil, but they move around South America like transients. They have homes in Argentina, Peru, Uruguay, Paraguay, and many other countries. They appear to be business people, which in fact they are. These families have been operating for at least three generations. And their main business interest: investment banking. They own or control at least twenty private banks in at least eight different countries."

I thought it would be a safe bet that Lieutenant Colonel Jeffords had obtained the million and a half to bail out one Clinton Davis, attorney-at-law, from this source.

Gallagher carried on: "The money at their disposal is not in the millions of dollars. It's in the billions. And their thirst for more is never quenched. With all that money comes power—or more directly, the ability to control those in power. Bribery is a commonly used tool, as well as blackmail and extortion. Anyone who gets in their way or whose loyalty is in question is rendered harmless; in other words, taken out. From our vantage point, it appears as though they don't have any political agenda. The principals in these families remain arm's-length away from the action. So our reality is that they are virtually untouchable. But we are getting closer."

I couldn't help but think about Clifford Parks and Gallagher's phrase *rendered harmless*. I noticed he wasn't consulting any notes.

"So how do they make their money? One might think that you can acquire a sizeable income in the investment banking business. And you can, but not these kinds of dollars. They started out as criminals, many years ago, and became bankers after the fact, not the other way around. They will sell anything and everything, regardless of the product or service. Drugs of every kind, illegal arms, chemical weapons, diamond smuggling, human trafficking, murder for hire—you name it, they're into it.

"Their MO is simply genius. They take the income generated by those activities and invest in legitimate, legal, aboveboard companies. Did you know that they are a three percent shareholder in Westlake Industries? And that's how your friend and mine, one Lt. Col. Karl Jeffords, became involved with the Group of Six. I'll get to that in a few minutes."

Mr. Gallagher knew his stuff and he was wrapping it all up in a neat package. Mel looked totally mesmerized. This was her world. It wasn't mine.

The background session continued: "How do they turn their ill-gotten gains into squeaky-clean investment dollars? They move the money around their various banks and offshore accounts, and like a magician's sleight of hand, those tainted dollars become as clean as new-fallen snow. They own, and I mean literally own, the watchdog agencies in those countries in which they operate. They function with impunity.

"Their public relations work is also beyond reproach. From the outside they appear to be family oriented and focused on social issues. In the name of their many companies, they build clinics and hospitals. They run food banks in poor areas of South America. Regular Robin Hoods they are."

Of course, I was thinking that these guys, the Group of Six, were brilliant. Keeping the law at bay and spreading their ill-gotten gains among the poor and downtrodden. Both sides of the fence covered. Indeed, brilliant.

Mr. Gallagher was far from finished. "So why was this task force created? There were some groups in the Middle East, terrorist organizations, who acquired some armaments that had once belonged to various military branches of the former Soviet Union. I'm talking rocket launchers, grenade launchers, surface-to-air missiles—all kinds of stuff, and easily acquired if you have the money. These terrorists shot down several of our helicopters, at least two of our F-18s, and blew up a building in what was supposed to be a secure compound, resulting in a great many casualties. Our guys.

"It took a few months, but eventually we were able to trace the sale of the illegal weapons back to the Group of Six. And the folks at our government's highest level said enough is enough."

Gallagher paused to take a sip of coffee.

I put my hand up. Not sure why I did that.

"I have a question, Mr. Gallagher."

It seemed he did not care for the interruption, but he let me ask it anyway.

"Just a thought, Mr. Gallagher, but if we don't want the bad guys, as in terrorists, to have all those Russian armaments, why don't we, meaning our government, go in and either buy them all up or we send in the special ops guys and destroy them all?"

He looked over at his two traveling companions.

"Not a bad idea, Mr. Simmons. All those options have been considered and, for whatever reasons, have been either discounted or abandoned or both. I assume international diplomacy would be at the core of those decisions."

Maybe I hit a nerve.

"Now, may I continue, Mr. Simmons?" he asked facetiously.

I nodded my approval, which he certainly didn't require.

"So, the task force was created. We have been gearing up for a major takedown for several months now. The government of Brazil has taken the lead to build a case against them, but it still will take some time for that to happen.

"Back at the ranch, what about here, in our country? The Group of Six owns and operates businesses worldwide. Up to this point they have only made investments inside our borders. Again, up until now, but they want to expand. The purchase of the Barclay farm, as you called it, Mr.

Simmons, is their first foray into actually operating a legitimate business here. Your opinion was that the reason they bought this property was ostensibly for the airstrip. You are spot-on. The cover business, as you suggested, is the Greenway Sod Company, and they will try to make a profit. They will have employees, pay taxes, all of the usual things companies do. Squeaky clean. They might even need a local attorney, Mr. Simmons. Hold that very thought for just a few minutes."

Of course, that statement sent my mind for a wild ride. Hold what thought? A local attorney? Did he mean me? I'm sure he was kidding. Then again, he didn't seem to be the kind of guy who would joke around with something like that. I wanted to put my hand up again, but I thought better of it.

He must have seen my eyes literally bugging out of my head, but he carried on.

"Alright, let's look at the landing strip. They will be able to bring in, by air, all kinds of goods, as I mentioned before. For discussion's sake, let's say they have flown in cocaine paste. It starts in South America, goes to the Bahamas or Jamaica or Puerto Rico, somewhere like that, and then comes into our country. Once it arrives at the Barclay farm, they will complete the process of turning the paste into powder or crack on those shiny tables you saw, Ms. Stockton, and pack the finished product into specially designed crates to be placed inside a truckload of sod, to then be delivered to their street-level distributors for sale to the end user. That's a much simplified overview, but it's pretty neat, huh, folks?"

Mel had a question but did not put her hand up.

"So why don't we simply stop this stuff from coming into the country in the first place? Any discussion about an airstrip on the Barclay farm would then become moot."

Mr. Gallagher gave Mel's question a little more latitude than he gave mine.

"Such a simple solution, Ms. Stockton. The truth is we stop about forty percent, estimated of course, of the drug contraband that is being smuggled into our country. That leaves sixty percent that we don't stop. So here we are, with our current situation.

"Good thought, but let's move on, shall we? How did we come upon all this information? The local stuff came from one recently deceased Clifford Parks. He had been recruited by his wife, the lovely and talented Dana Parks. Like a carrot in front of a mule, money beyond his wildest dreams was dangled before him. She told him everything, down to the last detail. She believed that she had him hook, line, and sinker. Her pitch to him was that they would help get the operation set up, then sell the newspaper and vanish into thin air, with millions of dollars in an offshore account, and live the good life forever. But she completely underestimated him, and in more ways than one."

I jumped in: "How on earth were you able to connect with Clifford Parks?"

Gallagher glared at me over his glasses.

"As I was about to say, Mr. Simmons, Mr. Parks had written a piece about meth labs in Dunham County, which at the time was a serious problem here. A really great piece of journalism, in my opinion. It was picked up by a national newspaper syndicate and that's how we found out about him. One of our target businesses in this country was the Pegasus Group. We'd had our eye on them for quite some time, and when we found out about their purchase of the land here in Lenore, we connected the dots and Mr. Parks was approached. Our timing was impeccable. He had just discovered that his wife was, shall we say, making herself available for extracurricular activities with Mayor Winfield, a little ten toes up and ten toes down. Without much pressure, he saw the light. In his message to you, Mr. Simmons, he spoke about their knowledge of your calls to the West Coast, so we have to be cognizant of the potential danger in which you may find yourself."

Way past "potential," I thought. I had told him about my bumper-car experience on Route 81.

His voice softened somewhat. "Let me say just one thing about Mr. Parks. Although he was initially taken in by his wife, I have never met a more honest, decent person in my life. The love that he carried for her was without bounds, but his sense of right and decency prevailed. And we owe him so much."

I wanted to stand up and applaud. And what we owe him can never be repaid.

Gallagher paused a minute, almost reverently, before he continued: "Before I go any further, I have a footnote to the Dana Parks–Warren Winfield affair. It's a ruse. We have had the principals under surveillance for quite some time. Dana Parks is stringing the mayor along. She is, in fact, having the real affair with the retired Lt. Col. Karl Jeffords. He stays at the Ambassador Hotel in King City when he's in town, which is becoming more and more often. She spends a lot of time with him in his suite, which we had the opportunity to bug a time or two. They weren't talking much about Pegasus, and what there was could only be described as pillow talk. I think Warren Winfield may be in danger, along with you, Mr. Simmons. He's simply a pawn, dispensable, a way to get what they need. Then who knows what will happen to him. I personally think they will keep him in place. They need someone at his level to ensure that their operations are left alone, without the undue burden of local government interference. My southern friends have a saying, 'If it ain't broke, don't fix it.' I think they'll leave him right where he is. If he gets out of line, mark my words, he will be taken along the same path as Clifford Parks."

I looked over at Mel and wondered if she was thinking what I was thinking. Was he serious about Pegasus needing local legal representation, as in me, and was Dana Parks spending more time on her back than on her feet?

It felt like Mr. Gallagher was coming around the clubhouse turn and heading for home with his rather lengthy, but critical, explanation of current events.

And what about our friend, the retired lieutenant colonel? That was probably easy pickin's for Pegasus. Karl Jeffords was angry, frustrated, and mostly broke. Like all of their other partners, they offered him more money than he could spend in a lifetime. And being shareholders at Westlake, I'm sure the Pegasus folks had opportunity to make his acquaintance. He then recruited the mayor, who in turn drafted Dana Parks and her husband into their close-knit, like-minded circle of friends.

"When I found out that you've been getting your nose into Pegasus's business, Mr. Simmons, I was admittedly furious. We could not afford to have our mission blown because of one local yokel lawyer in Lenore." He looked right at me. "No offense, Mr. Simmons."

"None taken, Mr. Gallagher," I lied.

"As you can see, Mr. Simmons, and you as well, Ms. Stockton, there is a much bigger picture, and since you're both now in that picture, I've got a plan that I will share with you.

"Alright, you have questions?"

So our new friend Mr. Gallagher had a plan. I bet he did. And I'd put up my firstborn as collateral, if I had one, to bet that somehow or other I would end up in the line of somebody's fire. I would hazard a guess that retreat, at least on my part, was no longer an option.

Having completed his lecture, Mr. Gallagher was soliciting questions. Mel and I stared at each other. I was completely overwhelmed, totally out of my element, and at that moment, incapable of putting all the pieces together. That was a lot of information to process. I knew at some point I would have questions, probably dozens of them, but none came to mind right then. Mel, on the other hand, had that look on her face. She was, in fact, putting the puzzle together. Her mind was probably moving at the speed of light. For me, the irreverent side had vanished, disappeared. Not one witticism. But funny thing, and to this day I can't explain it, as I looked at Mel, a sense of calm came over me.

Mel finally broke the deadlock.

"This sounds like organized crime from the fifties and sixties, Mr. Gallagher. You know, the Sicilian boys. Families running a crime syndicate."

"That comparison has been made many times, Ms. Stockton. Many times. Believe it or not, this is on an even grander scale," Gallagher replied.

At that point I had located my ability to talk.

"Two things, Mr. Gallagher. So you were afraid that what the A Team was doing would blow your operation all to hell?"

"Absolutely, Mr. Simmons. What's happening here in Lenore is like a gnat on an elephant. A very tiny piece of the puzzle. And the second thing?"

"Frankly, this is for my own edification, as a lawyer. I assume, along with surveilling Pegasus, you had the prestigious law firm of Davis, McLean, and Sewell in your sights. My question is how on earth did Mr. Davis escape jail time for dipping into clients' funds?"

He chuckled. More to himself, I think.

"Let's just say, we felt that Mr. Davis would be of more value to us and our operation enjoying the perks of freedom, rather than the limitations of incarceration. The judge cooperated. But make no mistake about it, Mr. Simmons, Mr. Davis's daily routine will eventually include peering through prison bars. That law firm is another wall that will come tumbling down."

As a representative of the legal community at-large, I felt satisfied that our Clinton Davis would, at some point, pay for those indiscretions, among other things.

I couldn't think of another thing to say. And it was all quiet on Mel's side of the table as well.

Now Mr. Gallagher was about to share his plan, which I feared included me being the local attorney for Pegasus. And that would make me, Brett Simmons, a double agent—a spy. John le Carré would add me to the list of Smiley's people. That didn't scare me, nope. Now I was terrified.

Gallagher continued, "So as far as the plan is concerned, and having shared with you all of Operation Rio's secrets, we are not asking you to volunteer. Too late for that. Should you choose not to participate we will hold you incommunicado, which is a nice word for holding you against your will, for as long as it takes for our operation to be completed. Years, I suspect. And for your edification, as you put it, Mr. Simmons, in cases like these, involving national security, habeas corpus does not apply. So I will assume that both of you are on board."

I looked at Mel. She looked at me. We both nodded our acceptance. Mr. Gallagher had a unique way of getting what he wanted.

"The last communication we had with Clifford Parks was a few days ago. He told us that the airstrip is on schedule to be completed next week, perhaps sooner. It will not be paved; gravel only. They want to try it out. A test run, in real time, so to speak. And it will be live. Two aircraft will land at the Barclay farm. One will be carrying nothing of interest, but the other will be carrying some product. Here's our dilemma: we don't know exactly what the product is, what type of aircraft will be used, which aircraft will be carrying the goods, and, most importantly, an exact date and time for the wheels to touch down. That's where you, Ms. Stockton and Mr. Simmons, come in."

And here we go.

Gallagher was looking directly at me. "Our benefactors do not want these drugs—or whatever the product is—to hit the marketplace. So we're going to stop this thing before it gets started. The entire operation, here in Lenore, will be run from your department, Ms. Stockton. We, Operation Rio, will be in deep cover. You will make the bust at the Barclay farm, take down the bad guys, and get all the credit. Again, Operation Rio does not exist. Understand?"

I fully expected Tom Cruise and his Mission: Impossible gang to come bursting through the door.

Mel's mind was on the operation at hand. She had concerns. I knew she would.

"We'll need some help to get all the assets we need in place, Mr. Gallagher. Not much time. Frankly, I'm more than apprehensive about this operation ending well, I mean, for us."

I wanted to yell at her, "Agent Stockton, I'm about to pee my pants!" Apprehensive? I should hope so. From my perspective, we didn't have a chance in hell of bringing this thing to a successful conclusion. *Successful* being defined as me sitting in my condo safe and sound and all the bad guys in jail. That was my inside voice. I bit my lip and remained silent. I didn't want to appear to be a weanie again, in Mel's eyes at least.

Gallagher responded, "You'll get all the help you require, Agent

Stockton. And yes, we have less than a week to put it all together. It's doable. It has to be."

She nodded. "Thanks. I've got some work to do."

There was a calmness about her. A confidence. Having seen how she handled herself at the Barclay place and now in this situation with so much more on the line, I felt a sense of pride and admiration. What shape would I have been in if she hadn't been there with me? I had never known anyone like her before. Never.

Gallagher turned to me. "As for you and your A Team, Mr. Simmons, I want your partners to continue doing exactly as they have been. From what I've seen, they've been providing you and Ms. Stockton with information in and around city hall. Am I correct?"

Mel and I both answered simultaneously, "Yes."

"Good. I don't want them doing anything different. Now here's the part that gets really interesting. I want you, Mr. Simmons, to infiltrate the Circle, to become one of them."

At that instant, my eyes must have bugged out of my head. Again.

All I could say was, "What?" Did he just use the word *infiltrate*? Yep, he did.

He continued, "They suspected Clifford Parks was about to impart their plans to someone. And that someone, Mr. Simmons, would be you. But we're not sure that they knew it was you. And at this point, we believe they have assumed that, with the removal of Mr. Parks, his information went with him; that he hadn't been able to share any details of their operation. And you, Mr. Simmons, will advise the good mayor, and only him, that their assumptions were incorrect and that Mr. Parks did indeed share everything he knew and you were the recipient of said information."

So let me get this right, Mr. Gallagher, my inner voice yelled again. Am I supposed to call the mayor's office, request an appointment, and over coffee, offer my services as a double agent? Sure.

The buffoon in me came back to life. I just blurted it out: "Are you *crazy?*" I did, in fact, believe he was.

He nodded in agreement. "Probably a little, but this will work. You'll operate under the guidance of some of my people. They'll get you ready for your performance."

Performance? Operate as in *operative*?

After Gallagher had outlined what he had in mind for a small-town lawyer from Lenore, I didn't feel any less stressed out. Again, sheer terror. But in a weird sort of way, it did make sense. And of course there was Melanie. So I had to either spend a great deal of time, as Gallagher had put it, incarcerated or place myself, side by side with Mel, right smack in the middle of Operation Rio.

Either way, I was at his mercy. Some choice!

CHAPTER 24

MR. GALLAGHER AND HIS two friends headed out before dawn to places unknown, leaving Mel and me sitting in my office, staring at each other.

Frankly, it would take a calculator to count all the emotions that were screaming through my mind. One for sure, I was not a happy camper. I decided to let Mel in on my emotional state.

"That went well, don't you think, Mel? You've been put right in the middle of doing things that you normally do, which is chasing bad guys and putting them behind bars, getting all the help you need from this nonexistent federal task force. Me, on the other hand," and by this time I was yelling. She let me finish. "I'm just a piece of meat attached to a hook about to be put into the water tank to lure some nasty man-eating sharks. And when I look around, I'm all alone. No backup. No cavalry. No posse. Just me, myself, and I."

I couldn't understand her calm expression. Like nothing was wrong.

"Yep, you pretty much covered it all, Counselor. Oh, and how do you like your vodka martinis, double-oh-seven? Shaken not stirred, I presume?"

"You, ma'am, are not funny. Not in the least."

I wanted so much to be mad at her. Then came that grin.

"You have to have a code name. James Bond. Yep."

"You are getting quite a good laugh at my expense."

She was, in fact, laughing.

"Sorry, Brett, I couldn't help myself."

"OK, Ms. Stockton, I'm trying very hard to maintain a decorum suitable for a double agent. So in keeping with that effort, I ask you, what's next?"

Half of me wanted her to stop smiling, and the other half would've missed it if she did.

She was way ahead of me in the planning department.

"I'm afraid we won't be spending much time together over the next few days. I'll be as busy as a one-armed paper hanger. I have to organize the takedown, making sure we have all escape routes covered. Not having a date and time is not working in our favor, and that's where you come in. But we do have the location and we know most of the bad guys already. And you will be spending some quality time learning the art of espionage from Gallagher's people. When did he say they would be arriving?"

"I think it's tonight. They'll probably show up covert and clandestine, quoting your friend Gallagher."

"I thought he was your friend, Brett." She was grinning again. "In the meantime, I'm going to assign one of my guys to accompany you wherever you go."

"So I'm about to have my own bodyguard? I thought that was you. So our live-in relationship is over?"

I already knew the answer. And I didn't like it.

"Brett, were you paying attention to any of what Gallagher said? You are probably in danger. These guys don't play around, and they would like nothing better than for you to join Clifford Parks, enjoying the cooler temperatures in the morgue, capisce?"

"OK, I got it. Listen, Mel, a comedian years ago once said that he felt like a pair of brown shoes in a room full of tuxedos. That's me. I'm so out of my element right now. I can dance around a courtroom like Fred Astaire, but I'm totally lost in your and Gallagher's world. Terrified basically describes it."

The grin was gone, and her voice took on a serious tone.

"I'd be concerned if you weren't afraid. Hell, I'm scared too. Fear is what keeps complacency from taking over. My brother—the airline pilot—once told me there are old pilots and bold pilots, but no old, bold pilots. If you stay on your toes, pay attention, and do what Gallagher's people tell you, you'll be fine."

I wasn't that confident.

She dialed a number on her cell phone and requested that an agent come to my office to "babysit" the lawyer. Yep, she said that, for my sake, of course. It was a little after 6:30 a.m. when she left.

I called Peel and told her to stay at home and that I'd explain later. I hated to do this to her, but I forwarded all of the office calls to her cell phone. As always, Peel was OK with it. There was no other alternative. I didn't need the extra worry of her being alone in the office.

And speaking of being alone—I was, for about an hour. While I waited for my newest, best friend, an AG agent named Wyatt, yep, as in Earp, I allowed my mind to wander to relieve some of the stress. It didn't help much.

If I was double-oh-seven, licensed to kill, as Mel so thoughtfully suggested, then I would need a Bond girl. I'm not sure if Carrie Kincade would want the job, but since this was my fantasy . . . We would, of course, be in some exotic place, say, the Bahamas, scuba diving in the morning, lunch at a waterside restaurant, playing baccarat in the evening. I'd be strikingly handsome in a white dinner jacket with a gold Rolex peeking out from under my French-cuffed silk dress shirt, and Carrie would be stunning in a sparkling gold lamé dress with spaghetti straps, looking totally in love with me. Then, after I won hundreds, no, thousands of dollars, we would go back to her place, a quiet little villa on a hill overlooking a bay with the calm salt water glistening in the lights.

I must have dozed off, because just as she said, "Oh, James," and was about to surrender to my charms, I heard a banging sound. It was Wyatt Earp coming to rescue me from the arms of a Mata Hari. Thanks, Wyatt. I owe you one.

Wyatt seemed like a pretty good guy, but young. It appeared that he had not yet celebrated his thirtieth birthday, which didn't give me the confidence I had hoped for. On the upside, we hit it off right away and that put me somewhat at ease. Thankfully, watching him check the doors and windows, he seemed to know what he was doing. He had thought about going to law school at some point, so he had lots of questions and that was good for me. It took my mind off of other pressing matters.

Neither of us had slept, so we decided to head over to the condo for some shut-eye. He was aware of the bug—or what Mel thought was a bug—in the condo. We decided that he would be the nephew of an old law school buddy, in town for a job interview. He was OK with me calling him Wyatt.

I wanted a code name and not James Bond. Thinking about my new friend Wyatt, I settled on Doc Holliday, although I didn't tell anyone. Whether I liked it or not, I was their Huckleberry.

CHAPTER 25

SO FOR THE NEXT FEW days I was at the hands of Gallagher's people, learning Espionage 101. And to say I was fast-tracked would be a major understatement. I had crammed for finals at college a time or two, but nothing like this. Not only did I learn how to shoot that black gun that goes bang when you pull the trigger, but I also became skilled at taking it apart and putting it back together again. Not sure why I had to learn that. My instructors' weapon of choice for me was the Glock 19, apparently the favorite handgun of modern law enforcement. Doc Holliday's Colt 45, or whatever he used, was no longer in production and therefore unavailable to his namesake double agent, me.

I had to practice putting on a bulletproof vest. When they first told me about my new clothing accessory, I envisioned a bulky, two- or three-inch-thick, extremely cumbersome and uncomfortable pullover that made me look seventy-five pounds heavier. Nope. It was almost wafer thin. Not sure how this thing would stop a lawn dart, let alone a bullet, or worse. My instructors assured me that it was the latest and greatest, and who was I to argue? Then, of course, there was the wire, as they called it; a wireless microphone that was taped to my body. I forced myself to wear the shoulder holster for my Glock as much as I could. All of my new accessories weren't particularly comfortable, but you know me, it's all about the job at hand.

They initially thought that I needed some lessons in bluffing. Not the kind you use at a Friday-night poker game in a friend's basement. Nope. It was what you used in undercover work, which was now my profession, although not exactly chosen. After a few sessions, I convinced them that as a lawyer I had been in the bluffing game for quite some time. I gave myself an A+ for that class.

Finally, there was the script. Not like a movie script, but basically an outline of what they wanted me to say and, of course, how and when to say it. There was some specific information I needed to gather, so we role-played over and over again. I think I got pretty good at it.

After four days and some consultations with my instructors, Gallagher declared that I was ready for my mission. I fantasized that I would be flown in a small single-engine plane over France, where I would parachute behind enemy lines to join the partisans in blowing up factories and rail lines. Exciting stuff. Who am I kidding?

I was not excited. This was not glamorous. I was in over my head and I knew it. If I screwed up—even just a little—there would be no way I could come out smelling like a rose. Fear often takes your mind to strange places and I found myself thinking about my funeral. Should I be buried or cremated? Yikes!

The waiting, like I have said before, was probably the hardest part for me. Although I was petrified, I wanted to get it over with. Get in, get out, and move on with my life. I yearned for a real estate closing, a divorce deposition, any mundane legal activity that I was put on this earth to do. I promised myself that if I made it through this, I would never again complain about my life as a lawyer. You know me. A promise is a promise.

Gallagher and Company had decided that there was a weak link and it wasn't our Portuguese-speaking friend, Carlos the Jackal, as Mel and I had decided. Nope. A much weaker link, according to Mr. Gallagher, someone else a little closer to home. And that was who they called "the target."

I had to be ready to move at any moment. I could expect no more than fifteen minutes notice. And the absolute worst thing about the waiting game: no alcohol stronger than mouthwash was to pass through my lips. My mind wandered back and forth between Carrie Kincade and Bud Light. I hoped I wouldn't have to choose. I preferred to think about having my left arm around her waist and my right hand around that pretty blue can. Is that too much to ask? After all, I was risking my life here and I think a reward or two would have been in order.

* * *

It was about seven thirty on our fifth evening together as roomies. One of Gallagher's associates, a wire-tap specialist, found the bug—or bugs, actually—placed in my condo. He didn't remove them. One was in my bedroom, one in the hallway, and one in the living room. He was able to place small white noise devices next to the bugs that would, as he called it, distract them, whatever that meant. So we were able to move around freely.

I didn't tell Wyatt, and nothing against him, but I missed Melanie Stockton. I pictured her going over details of the operation with her team. I was watching *The First 48* reruns and Wyatt was pounding away on his laptop when his cell vibrated. I immediately felt the need to throw up. I got the shakes. I was sweating profusely. I felt like I was on death row and the call was the governor denying my last appeal.

It was a go.

Wyatt taped the wire to my chest. I put on the bulletproof vest, a black shirt over that. I slipped into the shoulder holster and checked that the pistol was secure. We walked past the elevator and took the stairs.

We exited my building through the rear door, which, in all the time I had lived there, I had seldom used. It led to the garden, and we walked to the back of the grassy area, next to the bushes on the left side. We had rehearsed this several times, late at night, of course, to avoid any suspicions from my neighbors. Waiting on the side street was the black van. As we approached the side doors opened and Wyatt and I got in. The van headed east toward the Maywood district of Lenore. I knew where we were heading.

The Maywood area of town was definitely upscale. On Buena Vista Drive, a lush, tree-lined street, there wasn't a home under four thousand square feet or $750,000 in appraised value. The ordinary working stiff could not afford to live here. The "target" house was in the middle of the block, less than a ten-minute drive from my condo. We knew that the security lights came on automatically at dusk. There were no driveways. An alleyway behind the houses led to the multicar garages. The van drove down the alleyway and stopped at a predetermined spot, out of the range of the floodlights. Wyatt and I left the van and walked along the hedges leading to the garage. The van then headed back to the street to a designated holding place, far enough away to be inconspicuous and close enough to the target house to rescue a rookie double agent, should the need arise. You can guess how I felt about that.

I had memorized the layout, based on the information that Gallagher's people had given me. Let's just say they cased the joint on my behalf. So I knew that the side door got us inside the garage and a sharp left turn took us to the door leading into the house. Wyatt had disabled the alarm system and picked the locks. There hadn't been enough time for me to learn those skills. As soon as the interior door was open, Wyatt gave me a thumbs-up and headed back the way we came. He was to reactivate the alarm system.

I was alone.

Our target, well, mine now, had been under surveillance for several days. He did the same thing every night. He would park in the garage and enter the house through that same door. Once inside, one would be in a mudroom, just off the kitchen. Walking past the stove and refrigerator on the right, you would then enter the dining room, which in turn led to a sitting room and that's where I was supposed to position myself. The room was well lit when I first walked in, so I hit the switch and took a seat on a burgundy-colored, high-backed Queen Anne chair in the shadows. A little light was able sneak through from the dining room, so I wasn't in complete darkness.

And according to the plan, I waited. But not patiently, I'm afraid. I got up and walked around a couple of times. After I bumped into a coffee table I decided to stay put. I checked my watch, not the Rolex, but the Timex. It was 8:20 p.m. When would the target come home? Would he come home? I rehearsed my lines over and over again.

We had tested the wire. The recording devices were in the van and everything was in working order. I checked in every half hour or so.

"Doc Holliday, here—I mean, Simmons. Nothing yet." It was strange since they couldn't respond, and that left me with no idea if they had heard me.

As I have mentioned, waiting patiently was not a skill I had acquired, and probably never would. So for the umpteenth time I questioned my motives. Less a question and more a need to reconfirm what the hell I was doing here, and from a deeper psychological perspective, who I was and who I had become. From a professional perspective, there were no billable hours involved. The compensation, if any, would be nonmonetary. But I was really OK with that. I kept saying to myself, Brett, you know why you're doing this, so stop the self-analysis crap and move on. Of course I couldn't stop and I didn't. I thought about how Gallagher had recruited me, except that I was the one who got this ball rolling. You know, that first letter to Clifford Parks, that snowball heading down the mountain, which had become an avalanche. So I had to accept accountability for my actions. Was I crazy? Well, maybe a little. There's a definition of insanity: doing the same thing over and over and expecting a different result. I had never done anything like this in my life before and never wanted to again. So I checked the box indicating that I was, in fact, not crazy, just doing a crazy thing. And then my thoughts turned to Mel. I smiled. Absent this conspiracy, I would never have met her.

Right about then I heard the garage door open, and close a minute or so later. I checked my watch. It read 9:28. My heart started racing. My mouth ran dry. Inside the black gloves, my hands were clammy and started to shake. Get ahold of yourself, Brett. You got this. Yeah, right.

The door leading into the mudroom opened and closed again. There were footsteps on the kitchen floor, then on the dining room floor. A man was standing in the archway at the entrance to the sitting room. In his left hand he was holding a briefcase. With his right hand he reached for the light switch.

"No need to turn on the lights, Mr. Mayor. The ambience in here is just fine the way it is. Put the briefcase on the floor and take a seat. We need to have a little chat."

CHAPTER 26

IT DIDN'T TAKE LONG for me to discover that the mayor of Lenore was more afraid than I was. He tried to hide his fear, but he was unsuccessful. Initially he put up a bold front, but that didn't last long. And if I was to follow my brief training in espionage, you take advantage of that situation. And I did. I also found out that my penchant for being irreverent was a plus. Yep, being a veteran wiseass was going to help me fill in the gaps in my education as a rookie double agent.

As I recommended, he took a seat, opposite me. I believed the ball was in my court. "Relax, Warren. May I call you Warren? Of course I can. I'm holding a gun and you're not. A reasonable person would assume that this Glock 19 puts me in charge, wouldn't you agree? Given a choice I prefer this to the Glock 10."

During my wait time at the condo with Wyatt, I had done a little research on the Glock company and their various products. I'm glad I did.

I proceeded, "The Austrians sure know how to make guns, don't they, Warren? This bad boy shoots nine-millimeter cartridges, and if I shoot you from this range, it's going to leave a mark. Actually, I hate guns. They used to scare me, but when I noticed your crack police force carries them, I thought, Why shouldn't I?"

Gallagher's folks had determined that the mayor did not carry a gun. I had no reason to dispute that; after all, he did have a bodyguard.

He hadn't said a word, so I continued: "In case you don't recognize me, Warren, I'm Brett Simmons, attorney-at-law. And I'm the guy who's been that huge boil on your hind end. But honestly, I hope we can change that."

I was becoming more and more confident. He remained motionless and silent.

"Nice place you're got here, Warren. I haven't had a chance to take the twenty-five-cent tour, but I assume the rest of the place is at least as elegant as this room. Just walking in here every night must piss you off, big time. I mean, given that you're the mayor and all—and you know what they say about real estate: location, location, location—it's a great place to call home. Except for the fact that your wife's family paid for it. And your daughter's education as well. Oh, and I nearly forgot, they bailed you out a few years ago, barely a step away from bankruptcy. That has to hurt, Warren. A big hit to your ego—your manhood."

He finally spoke: "How did you get in here and what do you want?"

He was trying to take control of the conversation. I waved the pistol at him.

"Patience is a virtue, Warren. Mr. Glock and I will let you know, in due time."

He just stared at me.

"How do I know so much about your personal business? I guess you could say I'm your wife's lawyer. It's unofficial right now, at least until she decides to file for divorce on the grounds of adultery. And that's a when, not an if. Among many other things, she told me all about your personal finances—or lack of—and your dream of becoming your own man, money-wise. And I think that's admirable, Warren. Part of the divorce will be the removal of Anne's family's money tree from your back yard. I hope you have a plan to replace it. Actually, Warren, I know you do."

I paused to gauge his reaction. There was none that I could tell.

"I'm a goal setter too. But the way you're going about it might be . . . I don't know . . . illegal. But we'll discuss that later."

Now he engaged me, which is what I wanted.

"Do you know where Anne is right now?"

"I do."

"Where is she?"

"She's in a safe place, Warren. She's fine, not that you care. And so is your daughter and her boyfriend."

He pointed his right index finger at me. "I don't give a damn if you believe this or not, but I still care."

"Whatever."

I wasn't sure where to go next, so I figured it was time to put the hammer down.

"Sad, about your friend Clifford. Sad and concerning at the same time."

"I had nothing to do with that." He jumped right in with his denial, even though I hadn't made any accusations.

"Really? I beg to differ, Warren, and here's why. He was killed because some people decided that he could no longer be trusted. And you're in bed with those same people. You don't have to pull the trigger to be guilty of murder, or in this case, drive the car. He knew a lot and they were afraid he might share that information, but—and I hate to be the one to break this news to you—they were a day late and a dollar short. He had already revealed everything he knew to a former adversary."

He remained silent.

"And guess who that was, Warren? Me. Brett Simmons."

I could tell he was beginning to get impatient, squirming in his seat.

"Do you have a life insurance policy, Warren?"

He seemed annoyed by my question. "What? Yes, of course I do."

"Me too. Actually, I have two policies. One payable to my parents after I die. I've always wondered why they don't call it death insurance, I mean, since it's only payable after someone dies. And the other one is there to keep me alive. Yep. This is truly life insurance, Warren. Everything Clifford Parks shared with me is in writing. Upon my death, or even my disappearance, said information will be delivered to one Clay Bonner. You know Clay, Warren. He's the investigator from the attorney general's office who put your predecessor Mayor Marty behind bars. You should have joined your friend, but lucky you, your involvement in that scam fell through the cracks. And Mr. Bonner's people are currently looking into Cliff's demise, and along the way they're going to look into corruption at Lenore Town Hall, and that puts you in the crosshairs."

He was shaking his head. "You're bluffing, Simmons."

"If you say so, Warren."

He leaned forward in his seat to emphasize his point. "You've got nothing."

I didn't skip a beat. "Don't you just hate name-droppers, Warren? I know I do. But humor me for a couple of minutes while I lay a few on you. There's so many, I'm not sure where to start. You know that I'm aware of the illustrious law firm of Davis, McLean, and Sewell and of course your friends at Pegasus Financial Group. Oh, and I know this has been bugging you. It was me who left that phony message at Pegasus."

"That's not news, Simmons. You're not that clever." He was gaining confidence.

I ignored the verbal jab. "And that call to Chief Pryor regarding the whereabouts of the vehicle that ran over Cliff, well, Warren, that was me. Surprised?"

He looked away in disgust.

"Your little move to expropriate those properties on Route 81 was pretty clever. Eminent domain is a handy tool to have when you need to build an access road, and being head of the local government, you can make that happen. A road that will lead directly to the old Barclay farm. Nice property, by the way. Did you know there used to be a landing strip on the place? That might prove useful at some point."

He stirred in his seat, but did not respond.

"Moving right along, Warren. There's your newest, best friend: Carlos. You're aware he works for Pegasus. Well, indirectly. He works for the folks in Brazil who sponsored all this activity. He's supposed to be your bodyguard, but he's actually guarding their interests. But you knew that."

Again he stirred.

I knew I was making him more and more uncomfortable. "He was driving the car that killed Cliff. The one I called Chief Cal about. Same one that tried to run me off the road, not that you have any knowledge of that incident. Wink, wink. I know where it is. I have it. DNA from Carlos and Cliff are all over it. Am I getting warm yet?"

He wouldn't look at me when he responded. I fully expected him to ask how I came about all this information. But he didn't. He was too concerned about his own welfare to think that far ahead. "What does all this have to do with me?"

"Still talking, Warren. The Barclay farm will be renamed the Greenway Sod Company, and to no one's surprise, sod will be grown, harvested, and sold. A solid, profitable, tax-paying business."

He was about to speak, but I held my hand up in that "do not interrupt me" gesture.

I continued, "Well, except for one thing. That airstrip will be as busy as O'Hare Airport, with all sorts of airplanes carrying all kinds of goods, all of which are illegal, Warren. You know, drugs, guns, humans. Yes, Warren, human trafficking. And where does Pegasus get all their money to invest in this little enterprise? From the same place Carlos calls home: South America. Those same folks in Brazil I mentioned before."

He was still refusing to look at me. "Why are you telling me all of this?"

"I'll give you this much, Warren, you're persistent. There's two more players I want to talk about. Something about a man in a uniform, don't you agree? And it's Air Force blue, being worn by Lt. Col. Karl Jeffords, Retired. He's as dirty as the water flowing down the Mississippi River."

Again, looking at the ceiling, he reacted angrily. "Never heard of him."

I chuckled. "If you say so, Warren, but there are some photos, I mean, high-quality stuff, of you and your friend Karl in the lobby of the Ambassador Hotel over in King City, acting all buddy-buddy."

And that of course was a bluff, a little white lie. I bet the guys in the van were high-fiving each other right about then.

I still had more arrows in my quiver. "And finally, the reason that Anne will divorce you, Warren: Mrs. Dana Parks. You and the grieving widow have been—how can I put this?—an item, for some time now. And frankly, that in itself is the reason Cliff contacted me. He would still be part of your little circle of friends if you hadn't given in to the temptation and taken a bite out of the apple.

He started to squirm again.

And my final envelope: "Oh, and one last thing, I almost forgot. The tapes. Dana, when she was playing the part of the loyal wife, she talked incessantly about the plans, the farm, and of course the money. Cliff recorded most of it, Warren. Truthfully, I've only listened to a few of them. Your name and your level of involvement were mentioned on several occasions. And last time I checked—and remember, I am a lawyer—your participation qualifies you as a coconspirator. That carries a hefty amount of prison time."

Now that was a big lie. There are no tapes. That one might even drag a smile out of Paul Gallagher.

Again he was shaking his head. "I haven't done anything illegal, Simmons."

"Have you noticed, Warren, I'm ignoring all of your pleas of innocence? You asked me earlier why I'm here. I guess on the surface it appears as though I'm the outboard motor in this little cesspool. But actually, I'm here to help."

He grunted and said, "I don't need your help."

"Hear that, Warren? That's the sound of me ignoring you again. Over the past few days, I've been doing a lot of thinking. I don't want to end up like Cliff and neither do you. I could forward the information Cliff gave me, along with the tapes, the photos of you and Karl Jeffords, and of course the murder weapon, the Chevrolet, to Clay Bonner. They will arrest Carlos immediately, and to avoid the death penalty, he'll disclose every last detail. And you, Mr. Mayor, will go down, hard. And me too, probably, but for a different reason. The folks in Brazil don't have much of a sense of humor. They would probably follow me to the ends of the earth to exact their revenge."

I paused to gauge his reaction. Still he wouldn't look at me.

"So, I have a plan. Interested?" I continued.

"You keep waving that gun around, Simmons. Do I have choice?"

"Good point, Warren. So here's the deal. I become your partner, or more accurately, your insurance policy. I hold what I have close to the vest, and you get to complete your assignment with the Pegasus Group, all neat and tidy. Sound good?"

"And you're doing this out of the goodness of your heart." There was a distinctly disgusted tone in his voice.

"I'm a lawyer, Warren, I don't have a heart. No, I'll get twenty-five percent of your take, and the same from Dana. From where I'm sitting, I don't have to negotiate. I'm holding the cards. Actually I've got the whole deck."

The way he was shaking his head, he couldn't believe what I had just told him.

I smiled and continued. "So let's recap, Warren. I disappear, or I'm dead, and you go to jail, or maybe worse. I stay alive and well, and you guys get to keep seventy-five percent of three million dollars each. No brainer, don't you think?"

He laughed. "You're off on your numbers, Simmons. Two million each."

Got him! That sounded like an admission of guilt to me.

I wanted to jump up and down, but I retained my calm demeanor and went on. "I will open an offshore account, you make the deposit, then we'll all follow the yellow brick road. Once the money is there, I'll give you everything I have: notes, tapes. I'll even destroy the car."

He jumped in: "We don't have the money yet."

"Warren, you just said the wrong thing. We're done here. And when I say done, for you, it's game, set, match."

I got up as if I was going to leave.

He put his hand up. "OK, OK. We've got the money. In the Caymans."

I could picture Gallagher preparing the arrest warrants.

"That's the kind of cooperation I was looking for, Warren."

Finally he looked me in the eye. "How do I know you won't burn us?"

I showed him that confident smile. "Frankly, Warren, you don't. But if you give it a long, hard look, what other choice do you have? What is it they say, Warren? Gotta risk it to get the biscuit. And whether you like it or not, you have to trust me. After all, we'll be collaborators. Partners. On the same side. Which brings me to something else. As your partner, 'your' meaning both you and Dana, I have a need to know everything, down to the last detail. Every last one. Because if you hold anything back, I'll think you're cheating on me. Every detail, Warren."

He looked confused. "Like what? You think you know everything already."

And here's where I had to close the sale. Right there and right then.

"Cliff told me that the landing strip is almost ready. When are they flying in the first shipment of goods? How? What airplanes will they use? Where are the planes coming from? And when someone looks in that airplane, what will they see? Guns, dope, illegal aliens? See, Warren, all this strengthens my position and, at the same time, makes our relationship stronger. And I know you want nothing more than a deep-seated bond between us."

He looked down at his feet. "I don't have that kind of information."

"I'm sure our friend Karl Jeffords does. You can ask him. Or Dana can."

And now for the final nail in his coffin.

"Do we have a deal, Warren?"

What seemed like a very long time was probably about a minute.

I had him and he knew it. Dejectedly, he mumbled, "You said it. I don't have much choice, do I?"

"Despite what many of the good citizens of Lenore think of you, Warren, you are a wise man. And for the record, I was never here and we never spoke. The only other person who needs to know about our little arrangement is Dana. And frankly, I don't care if she likes it. One wrong move and she'll fry like you, Warren."

That made him angry again. "Don't worry about Dana."

"I won't. Please do me a favor. Tell her I'm aware that you both withdrew something under ten thousand dollars from your respective bank accounts, just in case you have to make a quick exit, stage left. I'm pretty sure that our friends, say, Carlos, Karl, and their associates would be perturbed to find out that you and your lady friend might be planning an escape. They want you around, and not because they like you, but you're the mayor and you've represented them well in the past. Once this operation is in full gear, they'll want you around to further protect their interests. Make sense, Warren?"

He shifted in his seat again. I was starting to love the study of body language. So much said without saying a word.

It was at this point that I decided not to advise Mayor Winfield that his main squeeze was playing the same game with Karl Jeffords.

I had to make my getaway, so after the mayor had removed all of his clothes, at my request, I took the handcuffs that were so thoughtfully provided by Wyatt and cuffed him to the door handle on the refrigerator, placing the key about two feet farther than he could reach. It would take him several minutes to drag the fridge that distance so he could free himself.

I was met in the alleyway by the van, and like thieves in the night, we disappeared into the darkness.

CHAPTER 27

I EXPECTED THE RIDE in the van to be at least a little celebratory. Nope. It was as somber as a funeral home. I thought I had hit a home run. A four-hundred-fifty-foot shot to right field at Dodger Stadium. C'mon, fellas. A little pat on the back? Nope. Not even a handshake.

As I had earlier that evening, I knew where we were going. Thanks to the good work of Brad Perryman and his real estate contacts, Mel had been able to set up a command center in a partially unoccupied office building at the southern edge of King City. She got the use of the entire top floor. This would be my first visit.

We turned into the parking lot and stopped near the loading dock. We exited the vehicle and walked through a side door. The elevator was either broken or they simply chose not to use it. The agents accompanying me were in much better physical condition than I was. They bounded up the stairs. I took them one at a time. They were not amused at having to wait for me at every landing. Eventually the sign indicating we were on the sixth floor appeared. They looked like they could do it again, like right then. Not their lawyer friend. I don't care who's in charge, this guy would be taking the elevator for the return trip.

The office was virtually empty. The previous tenants had apparently left in a hurry. And the cleaning service had obviously missed this floor during the routine execution of their janitorial duties. It was dusty and dirty. Papers, file folders all over the floor. Probably perfect for our purposes. Yep, I said "our." I found myself taking ownership of my involvement. I knew why.

The only lights were coming from an office in the middle of the floor, as far away from the outside windows as possible. The venetian blinds on the latter were closed. Judging by the number of finger marks on the panels, closing them took some effort. From the outside it would appear as though the entire floor was in darkness.

As I walked in, all conversation stopped and everyone turned to look at me. Staring at me were two guys I hadn't seen before, sitting at a table that held what appeared to be some kind of electronic equipment. On the other side of the room, at another desk, sat none other than Paul Gallagher. His two pals that I had met previously were absent.

Thirst was an immediate concern for me. I was jonesing for a beverage made with hops, barley, and yeast. All I could see was some bottled water on the floor beside Gallagher. I pointed to the water. "May I?"

He nodded his approval.

I chugalugged about half of it.

No one was saying anything. So I opened up the conversation.

"Are you going to listen to the tapes, Mr. Gallagher?"

"Why, Mr. Simmons? The tapes are for posterity. I heard your performance, live." He pointed to the table with the electronic gear.

Just then the door opened and Melanie Stockton walked in. "So did I, Brett," she said.

I was expecting a comment from someone. I got silence.

"Did you get everything you wanted, I mean, from Warren Winfield?"

Gallagher responded, "Pretty much."

Again silence. I was expecting some kind of reaction.

"Well then, if you're done with me, perhaps I can get a ride back to my condo."

"We're not done yet, Mr. Simmons."

I thought to myself that maybe Gallagher wasn't done yet, but I wanted my contribution to the overall operation to be complete. Finished. Done. I had no idea what other duties he had planned for me.

"If I'm staying, I could sure use a men's room right about now."

One of the agents from the van accompanied me to the restroom. Not sure if he was there for my security or to make sure I didn't flee the scene.

Once back in the office, I got the same treatment. Not a word from anyone.

Finally, one of the agents operating the electronic gear spoke up: "Leave the stuff here for now, Mel?" He was obviously working for her.

Gallagher responded, "Yes. We're not sure if Mr. Simmons has completed his mission."

I wanted to shout, "Oh yes I have, Mr. Gallagher!" But I signed that secrecy document and I wanted to spend the night in my own bed, not on a cot in a cell provided by some obscure government agency.

I endured a few more painful minutes of absolute quiet; then Gallagher stood up.

"Mr. Simmons, apparently my superior, the one who put the task force together, was much distressed at my decision to place you—and these are his words—in harm's way. His anger at my assessment of the situation, and your civilian status, was such that I felt he was on the verge of finding a replacement for his second-in-command, which, as you know, is me. However, your performance tonight has proved me right, and I thank you for that."

I assumed correctly that what he had just said was the closest thing to a pat on the back I would ever get from Mr. Gallagher.

"As you were on your way over here, I was able to relay to him, with as much brevity as possible, how you handled yourself and the end result of your chat, as you called it, with Mayor Winfield. He was pleased."

I thought I detected a faint smile on his face. I may have been mistaken.

"As I said before, your mission is not complete. However, there is one stipulation which I had to accept. Moving forward, Mr. Simmons, your work here will be strictly voluntary. If you should choose to walk away, you may do so with the caveat that you are still under the Secrecy Act, which you and Ms. Stockton and her people have signed. Understood?"

I nodded.

Gallagher continued, "We need the mayor to move that money in the Caymans, further cementing any case we may have against him. And we still need those important details. We know the why, the who, and the where. We are still hamstrung without the when and the how regarding those two test flights at the landing strip. Without that information, Mr. Simmons, we are peeing into the wind. So what I'm asking—"

I did what I assume few people would attempt: I interrupted him in mid sentence.

"I'm in."

"What did you say?" he asked in disbelief.

"I'm in. After all, Mr. Gallagher, I am Warren's new partner. And for those in this room who don't know me, this is my town. Lenore. I grew up here. I live and work here. Now, what do want me to do?"

Sometimes even I'm surprised at the words that come out of my mouth.

I looked at Gallagher. He was as stoic as ever. I looked at Mel. She returned my look briefly, then gazed down at her shoes. Probably a speck of dust in her eye.

"Alright, tomorrow, Mr. Simmons, you will call the mayor using one of the burners—you know, a throwaway cell phone—and give him the account number to a bank in the Caymans. It's a real account. Tell him he has twenty-four hours to wire the money into your account and get you the information you asked for tonight. Then you hang up. Don't say another word. Got it?"

"Yes."

"Good. I have other important things to take care of. I'm not sure when I'll be able to get back here. Ms. Stockton, you are still in charge. I need daily reports from you, at a minimum. Mr. Simmons, if you can get this information for us, we can shut down their operation here and focus on the bigger picture."

He picked up his briefcase and walked out.

A few minutes after he left, Mel spoke to her two agents: "Guys, I need a word with Mr. Simmons, in private. Please excuse us. Wait for us on the loading dock."

After the men left, she walked over to me and put her hand on my arm and gently pulled me toward her. Our faces were almost touching as we looked directly into each other's eyes.

She asked in a soft voice, "Are you alright, Brett? I was pretty nervous, with you never having been in this situation before, but you did great. I mean, way above what I expected. You got him to confess, basically."

"I'm fine. Really. But I am glad it's over."

"You bluffed your way through it, even with the gun and all."

"What do you mean, 'the gun'?" I pulled away from her.

"The firing pin was removed."

"What? Who did?" One minute we were almost embracing and the next I was yelling at her.

"It was Gallagher's idea. He didn't want you to hurt yourself or our weak link, so he instructed Wyatt to remove it while you were in the bathroom at the condo."

"You're smiling, Ms. Stockton. You may notice I'm not. Wasn't it you who told me you can't take a knife, or a letter opener, to a gunfight? I would have been just fine if you hadn't told me. I was just beginning to trust Mr. Gallagher. I thought I could trust you. Now I'm not so sure."

I could tell that I had hurt her.

"I'm sorry, Brett. I couldn't do anything about it. I didn't find out until later. It's not too late to back out. I'll give Gallagher a call and tell him you changed your mind."

"Is that what you want, Mel?"

"Not really. Well, maybe a little. I'm still afraid for you, Brett. But I also have a job to do. And if you can't trust Gallagher . . . or me, I would rather you walk away now."

"I'm sorry. I should never have said that." I had put my big foot in my big mouth. Way to go, Brett. "I was upset. I do trust you, Mel, implicitly." This time I reached for her arm, but she turned away.

"You didn't answer my question, Brett. Do you want me to make that call?"

"No."

She turned and touched my arm again. "Thank you, Brett. We really need you on this. I really need you."

I understood what she was telling me. Or maybe not everything.

She looked into my eyes. "You look tired. Go home and get some sleep. Wyatt's in the parking lot waiting for you."

I didn't feel tired. I wanted to stay with Mel, but I had to accept that at this point I would probably be in her way.

"Where will you be, Mel?"

"Right here. I have a lot of work to do and not much time to do it."

Just as I reached the door, I turned back to face her. "I wish you were still my babysitter."

I guess she hadn't been able to get that speck of dust out of her eye.

CHAPTER 28

MEL WAS RIGHT. I was tired to the point of exhaustion. Mostly from an emotional perspective. I went in, flying solo, did my job and got out. I expected a celebration, but that's a rookie for you. I shouldn't have. The job was not over, or even close to it. They don't give out trophies at halftime. I chalked it up as a coaching opportunity. And I still had so much to learn.

Along with the fatigue, I was jacked up. Nervous energy. Frankly, I was waiting for the post-trauma effect to kick in. Shaking, sweating, even crying. It didn't happen then, but I fully expected it to hit me at some point. After a couple of beers I started to calm down. I felt the need to sleep settling in. Wyatt had given me the burner phone and shown me the account number for the bank in the Caymans. We agreed that I'd make the call to Warren Winfield at 9:00 a.m.

After a quick shower, I finished off the second beer and went to bed. I tossed and turned for a few minutes, then turned on the light on the nightstand. I stared at the bottle of melatonin. I hated putting foreign chemicals into this temple that is my body. And before you say it, beer is not a foreign chemical. Bud Light is a domestic product. I had no idea where my sleep aid was made.

Although I had not come to any conclusion, I suspected that the melatonin was the cause of my whacko dream sequences. It seems every time I took it, I had a weird dream or two, or six. And what's even more bizarre, contrary to most folks who say they can't remember anything about their dreams, I remembered mine down to the last detail.

I decided that sleep was more important at that moment than my hesitation to put foreign chemicals inside me. I took one three-milligram tablet and I guess I fell asleep.

* * *

I could hear the shower running. Carrie Kincade had moved into the condo with me. Had I known she was going to take a shower, I would have joined her. I was all about water conservation. "Shower with a friend," was my motto. After I heard the water stop I saw the bathroom door open, and with a pink towel over her head and wearing my partially open bathrobe, there stood Melanie Stockton. I panicked. What in the world is she doing here?

"I love your wife's shampoo. It feels really good on my hair. I'm going to buy some. Oh, and I used your razor, hope you don't mind."

"You've got to get out of here, Mel. She'll be home any minute."

"But I want to meet her, Brett. What's her name . . . Mary? No. It's Carrie? That's a pretty name."

Just then I heard the front door open, and my heart leapt into my mouth. And thankfully, there was this beeping sound. It wouldn't stop. It was my alarm. And for once, I was glad to hear it.

Right then and there I made up my mind to buy some Sleepytime Tea. No more melatonin.

* * *

I don't recall ever telling anyone about my dreams. And I didn't this time.

"Sleep well, Brett?" Wyatt asked.

"OK, I guess. Needed some melatonin."

"I don't use the stuff. Gives me wild dreams. You?"

"Nope. No side effects for me," I lied.

Wyatt and I got to my office at eight thirty. I instructed Peel to work at home. I know she wanted to ask me what was going on, but she didn't.

At precisely 9:00 a.m. I dialed Warren Winfield's number. He picked up on the third ring but didn't say anything.

"Good morning, Warren. Get a pen. You need to write this down."

"Go ahead."

I gave him the name of the bank in the Caymans and read the account number to him twice, and I had him read it back to me.

"Warren, you've got twenty-four hours to deposit our agreed-upon sum into that bank account and to get me the flight information I asked for last night. No extensions. Twenty-four hours, Warren."

I ended the call.

So I had an entire day with basically nothing to do but wait. Eight hours for sleep and sixteen for whatever. I decided to call the A Team to check in. Wyatt suggested that it might not be a good idea, at least not until this was over. Getting to noon was agony. I had no idea how I was to make it through the rest of the day.

At twelve thirty Wyatt's phone rang. He managed a few monosyllabic grunts, then put the phone down. About thirty minutes later there was a knock at the door. I jumped about three feet in the air. Wyatt calmly walked over and opened the door. And there, bearing gifts, was Melanie Stockton. And the offerings she brought were a large pizza, a comparable salad, and a mixture of canned soft drinks.

"Anybody hungry?"

I wanted to give her a hug, but with Wyatt present, I decided against it.

"And starving for some company," I responded. "Don't get me wrong, I really like Wyatt. Not in a brotherly way, but more like a babysitter. In the last four hours or so he has given me more information about himself, his family, and his friends than I needed to know. And I have told him way more about me and my life than any other human being has a right to know. I may have to kill him."

"I'm sorry, Mr. Simmons, the complaint department is closed for the day. You'll have to come back," Mel said.

Wyatt had seen the Brett Simmons–Melanie Stockton Show before. "If you two are through with your little verbal skirmish, I'm starving. Let's eat."

And we did.

As soon as we finished cleaning up the lunch debris, Mel got ready to leave.

Trying to delay her exit for as long as I could, I asked her, "Did you get any sleep last night?"

"I did. We had rooms at this little motel down the street from the command center. I must admit, it was not quite as clean and sanitary as the office we're using."

"Sleep well then, Ms. Stockton?"

"We did. And 'we,' meaning myself and the various dead roaches I found in the bathtub."

"So you didn't sleep alone?"

And once again, my mouth had beaten my brain to the punch. I got one of those if-looks-could-kill looks from Mel.

"You went there, didn't you, Brett?"

"I did. Sorry." Actually I wasn't all that sorry. She was smiling and shaking her head in what I hoped was mock disgust with me.

"Strange thing. I had a dream about you. I don't recall many of the details, but you were definitely in it."

"Was I fully dressed?" I thought this might get a rise—in a good way. Nope!

"Hmmm. If you weren't, then it would qualify as a nightmare."

"Touché, Ms. Stockton."

She left without hearing the details of my dream experience.

CHAPTER 29

THE STRUGGLE TO GET through the afternoon matched the morning. Coffee. Then more coffee. We both hammered away on our laptops. Wyatt was probably chin-deep in law enforcement stuff. I was wading, ankle-deep, through solitaire. I must have played it fifty times. I was successful just the once.

Right before five o'clock Wyatt's cell buzzed. He picked it up. The only thing he said was, "OK," right before he broke off the connection.

"Your check is no longer in the mail, Brett."

"What?"

"You are officially a rich man. Your offshore account, and I know you have several, it's the one in the Caymans, it now boasts a balance of a million dollars." He put his pinky at the side of his mouth like Austin Powers.

I must admit that my sphere of influence was ever expanding. It seems if I spend more than a few hours with someone, they morph into a smart-ass, just like me. Case in point, one Melanie Stockton. She was pretty much straitlaced when I first met her; now she can verbally joust with the best of them. Although I do recall a brief confrontation with a chubby, squat Greek gentleman in a used auto parts store in King City, where she more than held her own, without any help from me. And now my new friend Wyatt. What have I done to him? He'll never be the same innocent, young law enforcement officer. I have turned him. And frankly, I liked it, and so did he.

I responded in kind: "Really, Dr. Evil? I have never been absolutely sure that Warren and Dana would do it."

"Me neither, Brett. So what are you going to do with your newfound wealth?"

"Like I'll get to keep it. You know, Wyatt, a million bucks doesn't buy what it used to."

"So I've heard."

"Alright, Wyatt, let's keep our eye on the prize. Back to important stuff. What do you want to do for dinner?"

He nodded in agreement. "I think we should order something in and eat it here. The bug in the condo makes me uncomfortable. Your office, at least right now, is more conducive to an enjoyable meal."

We ate Chinese, and at about seven thirty we went back to Château Simmons for the duration of the evening.

Sleep came fairly quickly for me with no liquid or chemical assistance. If I had a dream about anything, I woke up without a recollection of any carnal activity with Carrie Kincade or any kind of activity with Melanie Stockton. I had no idea why I included Mel in this. OK, I did have some clue. Probably my subconscious playing footsie with my conscious. After all, she did make one cameo appearance. One. And here I am, making it out to be a nightly occurrence. Was it wishful thinking?

* * *

From my office, as I did the previous morning, at precisely nine o'clock, I dialed Warren Winfield's number.

No answer.

I dialed it again. Same result. My anxiety kicked in.

Finally on the third attempt, the call was picked up. I put it on speaker so Wyatt could hear.

"Good morning, Warren. I was afraid you were avoiding me."

"This is Dana. Warren wasn't able to take your call."

"Everything alright, I hope. Do you have my information?"

"Do you know what they'll do to us if they find out we've given you this?"

"Do you know what I'll do if you don't give it to me?"

I'm sure she did. I could hear the rustling of paper.

"The planes are coming in tonight. Right at midnight, as air traffic control at the King City airport changes shifts. They'll be coming in from different directions. The first plane is a Saab 340. It will land to make sure everything is OK; then it will stay on the ground for about twenty minutes before it takes off again. The second plane is a Beechcraft King Air 350. Same thing. On the ground for a few minutes, then it'll take off again. We couldn't find out where they're coming from or where they're going after they leave here."

"Which one will carry the all-important products, Dana?"

"The Beechcraft."

"Thank you, Dana. I feel like our partnership is rock solid, don't you?"

She didn't respond.

"I look forward to a long and mutually rewarding relationship, Dana."

I ended the call and got a fist bump from Wyatt. He immediately called Mel and gave her all the information. After he hung up, he was visibly relieved.

"Mel says to tell you, 'Great job, Ninja Warrior.'"

Well, you could've knocked me over with a feather. I finally got an attaboy from someone other than myself.

"Know anything about airplanes, Brett?"

"Lots. You buy a ticket, go to the airport, and when they announce your flight, you get on, take your seat, they take off, and in a surprisingly short period of time, they land exactly where you wanted to go."

He shook his head. "No, Brett. That's airlines. I asked if you knew anything about airplanes."

"I'm a lawyer masquerading as a ninja, Wyatt. Information about airplanes is not on my need-to-know list. But I'm afraid you're about to tell me way more than necessary about how airplanes fly, aerodynamics, jet engines, blah-blah-blah."

He proceeded to do just that.

"Brett, the Saab is a passenger aircraft. Seats like thirty-five or forty passengers. It is not a jet. Twin-engine turbo prop. Doesn't need a long runway for takeoff and landing. Not sure why they would use an airplane that size."

"Can you repeat that, Wyatt? I want to write it down. I had a friend who owned a Saab once. A four-door. Korean, isn't it?"

"It's Swedish, Brett."

I think I knew that.

He continued, "The Beechcraft King Air, on the other hand, is much smaller. Twin engines, propeller driven, same as the Saab. In a passenger configuration, it seats about eight or ten, I think. In some wilderness areas, it's often used to haul a limited amount of freight."

"Or dope"

"That too."

"Well, thank you, Wyatt, for sharing your wealth of airplane knowledge with the class. It's recess time now, so we can all go out and play."

"I was in Junior ROTC in high school. Air force. Learned come pretty cool stuff."

"Ah, high school, Wyatt. Best nine years of my life."

Again, he just shook his head.

"So please tell me I'm all done. Once they round up the bad guys tonight, I can go back to practicing law."

I got no response.

"Wyatt, why aren't you telling me what I want to hear?"

He was putting his jacket on and motioned for me to do the same.

After we left the office, we headed north on Route 81. We had to drive right past the scene of the impending crime. Eminent domain had reached another stage. Those eight houses were now in varying levels of demolition. What a waste. I felt sad.

As much as I wanted this to be over, I knew where we were headed and I didn't mind it. As a matter of fact, I was happy about it.

CHAPTER 30

AT THE OFFICE BUILDING, once again, we took the stairs to the sixth floor. As we headed for the command center, I noticed that the place still had not been dusted and the trash hadn't been taken out. The landlord needed to be advised that a new janitorial service would not be a bad idea if the place was to be leased again. The current tenants wouldn't be here that long, so I wanted to believe.

When Wyatt and I entered the office I was surprised to find a lot of people. SWAT-type people, to be more precise. I scanned the room looking for Mel, but I couldn't see her. They looked like soldiers getting their final briefing before battle. There was definitely a dress code. I didn't get that memo. Black shirts with pockets everywhere, stuffed with all sorts of gadgets. Black cargo pants. Ditto for the pants. They were stuffed with whatever a SWAT person needs. Black military-style boots. Some of the people were looking at digital maps on tablets. Some were looking at the weather report. There were probably thirty people crowded into the room.

I walked toward the desk that Paul Gallagher had occupied on my first visit. There was a group of people standing around it. There were a few soldiers of the female persuasion that I didn't recognize. I was looking for one, in particular. I finally spotted the auburn hair falling from the black baseball cap. I noticed she was dressed the same as the others. I walked up behind her.

"Ninja Warrior reporting for duty, ma'am."

She quickly spun around. And much to my surprise—and I'm guessing to everyone else's—she gave me a long, not unaffectionate hug. If she had held me any tighter, I might have broken a rib or two. I got the impression that she was glad to see me.

"Officers, your attention please. I'd like you to meet Brett Simmons. Code name: Ninja Warrior. Without his participation, this operation would not be possible."

Most of them came up, shook my hand, and thanked me. I thought about handing out some business cards, if I'd had them with me. Maybe one or two of them might need some legal help down the road.

I guess it was late in the fourth quarter, with no chance for a comeback. The trophy was about to be awarded.

Mel took me aside.

"I wanted you here for a couple of reasons. Once it hits the fan over at the Barclay place, I want you out of harm's way. This is as safe a place as any for you. And secondly, I wanted the team to meet you."

"Where are you going to be when the action starts?"

"Probably right in the middle of it."

I looked directly into her eyes. "I was afraid of that."

She turned serious. "It's my job, Brett. This is what I'm trained to do, along with all the others here."

I knew that, but I didn't have to like it. "I don't know the others. I know you."

She grabbed me by the arm and dragged me out of the office, into another small, unused office near the stairwell. Her face was flushed, her eyes glassy.

"We need to talk, Brett. I don't know what's going on here, but it can't happen. I won't let it happen. Do you understand?"

I had never seen this side of her before.

"That's easy for you to say, Mel."

"No, it's not, Brett. It's hard, very hard. I can't deal with this right now. I have to focus on this operation and nothing else."

"I understand." What I really understood was the fact that while I was going to be all safe and comfortable with my babysitter in an air-conditioned office building, Mel was going to be in the line of fire—in some bad guys' crosshairs.

And when she said she couldn't "deal" with this right now, what did she mean? There was this aching somewhere in my being that made me so afraid that when she "dealt" with me, it would be to say, "Thanks, but no thanks, Brett. It's been swell, Brett, but I'm just not that interested in you." And there I go, thinking of myself again. She's going into battle and I'm feeling sorry for myself. I'm sure if someone were to look up the definition of *narcissist*, they'd be looking at my picture. Wait—I'm the least narcissistic guy in world. Must be that post-trauma thing sneaking up on me. My mind was traveling to places it had never been before.

As she turned to walk away, another speck of dust must have gotten in her eye.

Without looking at me, she said, "I'm about to hold the first of four briefings. You're welcome to sit in."

I stood alone for a few minutes trying to gather my thoughts and rein in my out-of-control emotions.

When I made it back to the office the briefings had just started. The planned raid was code-named Operation Propeller. This first briefing went over the role of the helicopters. The second concerned the role of the armored personnel carriers. And the third dealt with establishing and maintaining a perimeter, to make sure no one slipped through the cracks. The last briefing—which to my mind was the most important—was about extraction, getting all these people out of there unharmed. I didn't miss the reference to the medical staff who would be close by, just in case. I couldn't even think about that.

There was as much detail as you could imagine. Every facet of the operation was discussed. The most important aspect of the planning was the timing. If any part of the raid were early or late, it could put the entire operation out of synch and its overall success would be in jeopardy. I heard someone say, "In and out, should be under fifteen minutes."

I was now even more concerned for Mel's welfare. Concerned, hell, I was scared out of my mind for her. I couldn't get my head around my damned emotions. OK, I was scared for us, whatever "us" meant.

In contrast to the previous day, this one went by very quickly. After the fourth briefing, I walked over to the outside window and peeked through the blinds. It was almost dark. The countdown had begun.

The command post for the raid had been moved to a mobile center impersonating a broken-down motor home set up closer to the Barclay farm.

The only ones left in the now eerily quiet, original command center were the two technicians sitting with the electronic gear; Wyatt, now babysitting the phones; and the one whose code name was Ninja Warrior.

CHAPTER 31

FOR WHAT SEEMED A very long time the place was strangely quiet. I could hear the two communications guys talking into their microphones, obviously responding to what they were hearing on their headsets. I could only decipher a word or two here and there.

Finally the larger of the two turned around and announced that everything was in place. I checked my watch, it was 9:41 p.m. Again, the waiting game.

Strategically, the plan was simple. The details, not so much. Tactically, probably just after midnight, the first aircraft—the Saab—would be allowed to land and take off again. It had been assumed that this would be to test the landing strip, among other things. Operation Propeller would be activated after the second aircraft, the King Air, which supposedly would be carrying the goodies, had landed. Once that had happened, the Saab that had just taken off would be intercepted by four Air National Guard F-15 Eagles. The Saab would be forced to land and the pilots would be taken into custody, hopefully, without incident. The

King Air would not be allowed to take off again.

Four helicopters would hover over the property with powerful floodlights illuminating the entire area. Loudspeakers on the choppers would announce to all those on the ground below that a police raid was in progress. The bad guys would be instructed to drop their weapons and lie facedown on the ground.

The front gate facing Barclay Road would be breached and three armored personnel carriers, with twenty-five heavily armed officers each, would speed down the drive toward the airstrip. The officers would exit the vehicle and begin to spread out, heading toward the plane, which would most likely be parked near the rear of the barn.

SWAT team members would be spaced about one hundred yards apart around the perimeter of the property, just in case any of the bad guys decided to flee.

The more I thought about it, fifteen minutes might just be enough time to wrap this thing up.

At about 11:45, I was offered a seat next to the communications guys, along with a headset. The chatter was beginning to pick up. I don't know who we were monitoring. Maybe the helos or someone on the ground. I had no idea.

Just after midnight, I heard, "Bird One on the ground." I knew that was the Saab. About twenty minutes later, "Bird One just took off. Stand by for Bird Two."

There was a strange silence. Three minutes went by. Then four, then five. Maybe the good guys had been made and the King Air wouldn't land. It had now been twelve minutes since Bird 1 had taken off. Silence.

Finally, a different voice came over the air. "Bird Two down. Go! Go! Go!"

My heart was beating out of my chest. I looked at my watch. Fifteen minutes.

A few minutes later I heard the words I'll never forget: "Ambush! Ambush! Get down."

All hell was breaking loose. I could hear gunfire and yelling. My headphones were about to blow up. And then came the worst: "Officers down! Officers down!"

How could this be happening? It should have been simple. Fifteen minutes and done.

I have no idea how long it took, but one of the communications guys looked at me and said, "It's all over. Secure."

"It's not over, it's not!" I was yelling at him.

The words "officers down" echoed in my head. I thought my brain would explode. Melanie Stockton was too good at her job. She would never take unnecessary risks. I know she's going to walk out of there.

I thought about my grandmother. She would know what to say at a time like this. It was over. But not for me. It wouldn't be until she came through that door.

I kept looking at Wyatt. The phones would ring and he would answer. I couldn't hear his responses.

After one of the calls, he hung up the phone and got out of his chair and walked toward me. He was holding back tears. Oh, my God.

"Melanie was hit, Brett. They're life-flighting her to a hospital. Not sure which one."

"Is she alive?"

"I don't know, Brett. I don't know."

"Give me the keys to your car. I'm heading to King City Memorial. It's the closest. Call me if you find out they're taking her somewhere else."

I knew it would take about forty minutes to get there—the longest forty minutes of my life. I tried to think positive thoughts. I hoped the Life Flight pilot was David's brother-in-law, Drew. He'll get her there in time. What about her parents and her brothers? I don't know how to contact them. Clay Bonner would know. She was doing what she loved. She was made for this.

I was a mess and I knew it. My mind started playing the blame game. If I hadn't . . .

Finally I saw the sign "King City Memorial Hospital." It seemed there were ambulances everywhere. I looked up to see a chopper taking off from the rooftop landing pad. Another was hovering overhead waiting to land.

I parked the car and ran through the Emergency entrance.

CHAPTER 32

AT FIRST, HOSPITAL SECURITY wouldn't let me past the waiting room. Then I spotted one of Mel's team members and he recognized me.

"Melanie Stockton. Is she here? Did she make it?"

He was out of breath, maybe in shock.

"We came around the corner of the barn, and they were waiting for us behind one of those earth movers. I have no idea how many there were or how they got there. We didn't see them until they opened fire. We lost three of our guys and she took four rounds. Two got her in the Kevlar vest. One in the left arm, just above the elbow. The fourth one got her in the thigh. She's lost a lot of blood. She's in surgery."

As he headed back down the hallway I sat down in the waiting room. I felt helpless. I couldn't stop her from doing her job and now I couldn't help her. I couldn't even cry.

Then I heard a familiar voice. It was Clay. He was trying to get past security. He had been in the mobile command center.

When I shouted at him, he turned and saw me. They were about to let him through and he waved at me to go with him.

It was a long night. She was in surgery for several hours. Clay was able to contact her parents and updated them every half hour. The doctors told us the bullet that hit her arm just above the elbow did significant, but repairable damage. But it was her leg I could tell they were concerned about. That bullet, probably a different caliber, they said, than the one that hit her in the arm, had smashed her femur and a bone fragment had punctured her femoral artery. Although she had lost a significant amount of blood, the work of the EMTs at the scene had saved her life.

It was daylight before they took her to recovery and several more hours before they would allow visitors. Only one at a time.

Clay went in first. He stayed about five minutes, and when he came out he was wiping his eyes.

"She asked for you, Brett. Wanted to know if you were here." His voice was cracking.

I entered the room and slowly approached her bed. There were tubes, it seemed, everywhere. Her left arm was heavily bandaged. Her right leg was elevated slightly. I had an enormous lump in my throat. Her eyes were closed. All I could do was stare. When I took her right hand, she opened her eyes and looked up at me.

"Hi." It's all I could say.

"Hi. How did you get here?"

Her grip on my hand was surprisingly tight.

"I stole Wyatt's car."

She smiled. "Clay said we got them. All of them." She started to cry. "Clay said we lost some of our people. I feel so bad. I worked side by side with them. I knew them. I know their families."

I put my finger to her lips and tried to change the subject.

"You're in great hands here, Mel. They'll take care of you."

Just then a nurse came in. "She really needs to rest, sir."

As I got up to leave, Mel touched my arm with her right hand. "Promise me. Promise . . ." Her eyes closed and she drifted off to sleep.

I had already made a promise. To myself.

EPILOGUE

AS I SAID AT THE beginning, that was nearly a year and a half ago. I guess you could say things have settled down, but they will never be normal again. Or whatever normal used to be.

What started out as two innocuous words of legalese somehow turned into all this. Eminent domain. How could anyone have known?

Regardless of the fact that I had been issued a code name, which I believe was more tongue-in-cheek than tactical, I was still a civilian, as so designated by Paul Gallagher's boss, whoever that was. I was not entitled, legally or otherwise, to read the report, nor should I have been privy to its contents.

The day after the raid, I was still under the watchful eye of Wyatt at the condo when a fellow agent delivered a package. He opened it up and handed it to me. He advised me that I had thirty minutes to read it. The agent would wait. It was the initial report on Operation Propeller.

Much of the information I was already aware of since I was involved, to put it mildly. The thing that bugged me more than anything else—

and I wasn't alone in this—was how wrong the intel was on the Barclay farm. Everything pointed to the place being occupied by a few workers and a handful of security guys, probably reporting to Carlos. Where did these twenty well-armed and apparently well-trained militia guys who ambushed Mel and her people come from? Simple answer: They were flown in on the Saab 340 along with a few additional farmworkers. All of those workers were Honduran, had entered the country illegally, and more than likely were forced to leave their homeland under some kind of threat—which was right up Pegasus's alley. So when Melanie and her guys came around the corner of the barn, surprise. And not in a good way. The guys overhead in the choppers had no time to react and warn the agents below. And that's when Melanie got hit and the other three agents lost their lives. I remember Wyatt telling me that it could have been a massacre. I thought it was. The good guys were able to regroup. The bad guys, realizing they were outmanned and outgunned, did the smart thing and surrendered, but not before several of their group were either killed or wounded.

Speaking of the Saab, when the fighters forced the plane to land, the only occupants were the two pilots. Sitting in the left-hand flight-deck seat, that being the captain's, was one Lt. Col. Karl Jeffords (Ret.). What on earth possessed him to participate in this little adventure is beyond my capability to understand. If he had just stayed away, I'm not sure there would have been enough evidence to arrest him, let alone convict him. Law enforcement officers were killed. And due to his involvement, he was formally indicted on—among other things—multiple counts of murder. He accepted a plea deal, which took life without parole off the table, not that it matters. At his age, he'll more than likely die in prison before he qualifies for parole. Couldn't happen to a nicer guy.

Wyatt's question was answered. He couldn't figure out why an aircraft the size of a Saab 340 was used. And now we know.

The second aircraft, the King Air, was chock-full of cocaine paste. I don't recall the exact amount in kilos, but the estimated street value of the final product would have been in the millions. Apparently, the Hondurans who arrived with Pegasus's troops were experienced in the art of converting cocaine paste into a street-salable product. Pegasus thought of everything, didn't they? Well, not quite. Why they didn't simply make this a dry run, I'll never understand. I guess greed will make really bad decisions appear to be wise.

At some point during the chaos that night, Jeffords was able to contact Dana Parks, who, of course, he thought was his main squeeze. As it turned out, that was the ruse, not the other way around. She was using him to gain a stronger footing in their operation. Her guy was always Mayor Winfield. So after Mrs. Parks was advised of the situation, she and the good mayor took a few personal things, along with some spending cash, which was the money they had withdrawn from the Lenore Bank and Trust, and quickly headed out of town. They drove almost three hundred miles to Wendover. It was at the airport in Wendover that they discovered, much to their chagrin, that their passports had been canceled. They were taken into custody.

There was a lot of detail in the report that I skimmed over. The Ninja

Warrior was not mentioned. I didn't need the notoriety, code name or not.

As for the happy couple, Warren and Dana, they agreed to testify for the prosecution. So with solid legal representation, and in return for that good deed, they were offered a plea deal, which they accepted. The good mayor of Lenore got twenty-five to life with the possibility of parole. Mrs. Parks received thirty to life with the possibility of parole. As part of the plea bargain, they relinquished the $2 million each in the Cayman bank account, less the 25 percent that they gave to me, of which I never even got a sniff. With Warren's bills being paid by the government, he won't need any of Anne's or her family's money any longer. I doubt they'll ever get comfortable in prison or anywhere else, what with the constant looking over their shoulders to see if the Group of Six has discovered their whereabouts. Disloyalty comes with an enormous price.

Then there's our friend Carlos the Jackal, aka Rambo. When the choppers arrived and ordered everyone to give themselves up, he was one of the first to lie flat on his stomach and surrender. Honor and loyalty—not an ounce of either in Carlos. He offered to assist the prosecution regarding the demise of Clifford Parks, but his help wasn't necessary and was summarily declined. With the evidence taken from the late-model Chevrolet, he was found guilty of the hit-and-run murder of Clifford Parks. After he serves his sixty-year sentence, if he lives that long, he'll be deported back to Brazil. There's a special place in hell for people like him.

The integrity of the federal task force and Operation Rio was maintained. And for that reason, the law firm of Davis, McLean, and

Sewell along with the Pegasus Financial Group and its assets were left untouched. For public consumption, the news gave total and exclusive credit for the success of Operation Propeller to the attorney general and his personnel.

But now, as I said at the beginning of our conversation, things have changed. Operation Rio is out of the bag. Basically, Carlos spilled his guts about Pegasus and his Brazilian employers. Apparently, he knew a lot more than a bodyguard should know. Of course, the mayor and his lady shared everything they knew, which really, when you look at the bigger picture, wasn't all that much. The main source of information was the retired air force lieutenant colonel Karl Jeffords. It was his knowledge about Pegasus and its backers, which he imparted to Gallagher's people and which was the main cog in his plea deal, that set the wheels in motion. Again, I have no idea why Jeffords was in charge of anything. He was a moron.

About ten months after Operation Propeller, once all this information had been shared among the stakeholders of Operation Rio, various agencies, led by Brazil's National Police, and with the necessary warrants in hand, conducted raids in several countries. Dozens of people were arrested, including many in highly placed governmental positions. Assets, in cash and other forms, were seized. By all accounts O Grupo dos Seis was rendered harmless. But there's a part of me that believes they still have a pulse, probably weak at his point, but a pulse nonetheless.

And what about my A Team? I'm so proud of my friend David Spencer. A wonderful husband, an amazing father, and now the mayor of Lenore. He is right where he needs to be. Brad Perryman continues to represent the good citizens of his ward, and he is David's most trusted advisor in his additional role as vice mayor. Bow Tie retired from public life. Well, sort of. With the help of some generous donors, including Westlake Industries, he established the Lenore Museum and Historical Institute, which is housed in the old Merrifield building, now known as the Clifford Parks Memorial Center.

Right against might. That would have made a great headline for the *Lenore Gazette*. Unfortunately, the paper remains unsold and is currently dormant.

There was a brief funeral service for Cliff Parks. His ashes were taken by a second cousin to a small town on the East Coast. I often think about Cliff. His courage. His conviction. He was a very brave man. In my mind, he will always be my friend, even though we never got the chance to cement our friendship.

I have never been able to find out for certain why all the secrecy around the seizure of the properties, the purchase of the Barclay farm, and even the repair of the landing strip. There was no need for all the cloak-and-dagger stuff since none of it was illegal. The best I can figure is that Lieutenant Colonel Jeffords, since he appeared to be directing the show, decided to make it far more difficult than it needed to be. If he had left it alone, instead of micromanaging the entire operation, I never would have taken things any further than being that blemish on the mayor's behind. I would rack that up as dumb crook news.

What about the women in my life? Honestly, I don't think my ex,

Sarah, would even know or care if I had left Lenore. And I'm OK with that.

I don't think Carrie Kincade will be lonely for very long. She's intelligent and beautiful and has a great sense of humor. Let's face it, she dated me, didn't she? I mean, about her having a sense of humor, not about her being intelligent. And to top it all off, she's a damned good lawyer. She took care of herself before she met Brett Simmons. I don't see anything changing from that perspective.

And then there was the very shallow reason I returned to Lenore after graduating from law school. I had to show Mallory McCutcheon what I had become and what she was missing. Our brief fantasy affair, well, my fantasy affair was just that. Dreaming about her was as close as I'll ever get. For many years I had no idea where she was or what she had become. My memories of her were based on a time when she was a sixteen-year-old high school sophomore. Recently, I found out that she married a Baptist missionary, and along with their seven children, they are spreading the Good Word in the wilderness of Tanzania. Good for them.

Now, I come to Melanie Stockton. I will never forget the night that my face was "this close" to her beautiful behind, or watching her verbally assault George the Greek, but mostly the sight of her lying in that hospital bed, having escaped the Grim Reaper by a matter of minutes. I will always be grateful to the wonderful doctors and staff who saved her life. And in many ways, mine as well.

It was a long recovery. She regained about 90 percent use of her left arm. That may be her new 100 percent. She has a slight limp in her right leg. The physical scars will be lifetime reminders of that night.

Due to her injuries she knew she would be unable to return to active duty on the front line. She was offered a disability retirement or a desk job as an investigator in the re-offender program.

The Group of Six, as I mentioned, did not play well with others. If you got in their way, you were eliminated. I got in their way. We couldn't know, at that time, if they were aware of me, or my level of participation in Operation Propeller. In conversation with Paul Gallagher, he said that he strongly believed that they knew and we needed to act accordingly.

Within days after the raid on the Barclay farm, I was entered into the Witness Protection Program. The perceived potential threat to my life was deemed substantial. I was given a few hours to pack some things and I was gone. There was no opportunity to say goodbye to Clay, David, Brad, Bow Tie, Judge Jimmy, or, of course, Peel. I miss my friends. Every day.

My current situation is both ironic and sad. I invested so much of myself and risked literally everything to protect my Lenore and, ultimately, what I thought would be my life there. But I can no longer go back. But no matter what, Lenore will always be my home. Ironic and sad.

I know this is a well-worn, over-used expression, but somehow it fits. When life gives you lemons, you make lemonade. I did.

I said that I had made a promise to myself, and I have tried to live up to that promise. I agreed to enter the Witness Protection Program on one condition. Once Melanie was physically able, if she so chose, I wanted her to join me, wherever that might be.

Life is good, considering it could have been a solitary existence. I'm no longer that person I once was. I no longer practice law. I'm no longer Brett Simmons. She is no longer Melanie Stockton. At least on paper.

But we are together. Even when we put all these events in perspective, and tragic as many of those things were, the human spirit allows us to move on with our lives.

If I had to do it all over again, I would. I have but a few regrets.

* * *

I almost forgot. What about Paul Gallagher? To look at him, he looked like a heart attack or stroke waiting for a time and place to happen. Both Melanie and I hoped he would retire. Then, the strangest thing happened. Last night, late, my cell phone rang, and as instructed by my WPP handler, since I didn't recognize the number or the area code, I let it go to voicemail. It was from Paul Gallagher and it was classic Gallagher. "Simmons. Call me. Gallagher." He left his number. What would he want after seventeen months? And he called me by my former name. Hmm. Probably to thank me, and Melanie of course, and to tell us what a great job we did, and we are forever in his gratitude, and maybe someday we could all get together for a drink. You know, for old time's sake. Sure. Probably not. I'd be surprised if he called his mother on Mother's Day.

I decided not to return his call. If it's important he'll call back.

ACKNOWLEDGEMENTS

THERE ARE SO MANY people I want to acknowledge with heartfelt gratitude, without whom, this book would never exist.

FIRST AND FOREMOST, MY family. To my wife, Janet, and my two sons, Adam and Alex, in Tennessee. I could never have written this without their love and never-ending support.

TO MY FAMILY IN Canada; my parents, Carmen and Primrose, for allowing me to follow my dreams; to my brothers and sisters and their families. Family is what holds all of us together.

TO MY BELOVED HOMETOWN of Ancaster, Ontario, Canada, and all of my wonderful childhood friends. As Brett Simmons states, I grew up in Mayberry. No matter where you end up, there is that one place you can always call home. Without Ancaster, there would be no Lenore.

TO ALL OF THE musicians and songwriters I have had the pleasure to work with, along the way. My first passion was music. My first original story was written in the Key of E.

AND FINALLY TO MY friends and partners at Indigo River Publishing. To C.E.O., Bobby Dunaway, whose leadership has Indigo River poised for many years of success. To all the professionals on the Indigo team. To my editor, Josh Owens, I will be forever grateful. He took this 'sow's ear' novel and turned it into a 'silk purse'. To Regina Cornell, copy editor, who made it look like my education wasn't a waste of time. To Emma Grace, book designer, who turned this field of overgrown brush and weeds and turned it into a delightfully landscaped portrait. And lastly, to my friend, Georgette Green, Acquisitions Manager. I will never be able to fully show my gratitude for her guidance, nurturing and grace.

RDD

CPSIA information can be obtained
at www.ICGtesting.com
Printed in the USA
LVHW010713020222
709616LV00001B/4